I0601649

Addition Jones

By Patsy Stanley

© Patsy Stanley 2019
The content of this book is fiction
and is fully protected under
copyright. No portion may be
reproduced in any form at
any time or through
any media without the
authorized consent
of the author Patsy Stanley
or her representatives.

ISBN 978-1733737173

Library of Congress Control Number:
2015904772

"Never set a child afloat on the flat sea of life
with only one sail to catch the wind."

D.H. Lawrence

Table of Contents

Prologue

He rode his horse through the warm spring afternoon and into the dark night without stopping, the bundle tied around his waist with the white sheet he'd stolen from her laundry basket. In random moments, when the tension built up and became too much, he cursed her and drank deeply from his bottle of whiskey. *This would teach her a lesson she'd never forget!*

Now and then, in moments more haphazard than random, he patted the bundle and laughed drunkenly at the dark fate he was handing her.

Dusk came and he saw a buggy path leading off the weedy, unknown trail he was following. He followed the path until it led down into a farmyard. He veered from the path and rode on, searching the overgrown fields until he topped a hill above the farmhouse.

He took another drink while he studied the farmhouse below. The rush of drunken, fearful joy was fading, and he was getting damn tired. He still had a long way to go before he reached home. He fingered the bundle. He was tired of carrying the damn thing. This place would do just as well as any other. She was damn lucky he didn't leave it under a bush somewhere.

He would have, too, if he wasn't afraid of getting into worse trouble. He studied the landmarks so he would remember where the farm was before he rode down the hill, dismounted, and laid the bundle up against the front door, mounted his horse, and slipped away into the gathering darkness.

Chapter 1. Addition Jones

Subtraction
Multiplication

"Add, subtract, multiply!" That's what me and my friends yelled from a goodly distance whenever we saw Addition Jones.

I figured Addition Jones was always an old man, for I could never picture him any other way. He looked like a tall, skinny scarecrow dressed in black clothes that hung like rags. He had heavy brows, black eyes, a hawk's nose, and a wide, turned down mouth. His cheekbones stood out like knife blades in his long, dark scowl of a face.

He was taller than most men. He had the biggest, boniest hands I ever saw. His snow white hair laid straight across his forehead like it was leading him somewhere, and nothing better get in its way. My friends and I hollered, "Old Add!" at him and took off running whenever he came around.

Dad would have given me my first whipping if he'd caught me at that little piece of meanness. The townspeople were careful to behave decently around my father; they said he was a man with too strong a conscience. I asked him what that meant when I turned ten.

In an even, exhausted tone, like it was a subject he'd worn out, he said, "There are countless other ways of being a better person than religion teaches us. Better to listen and learn from the good rules you carry inside yourself than to limit learning to any religion. Being human is not always an easy thing to deal with, but it's the best we got."

"Then why do you go to church?"

"Your mother."

"Oh."

I knew he would do anything he could to please her.

"Me too," I admitted, though I wasn't sure what I meant.

We both stared at the ground a minute, him for his reasons, me for mine, before we turned and went our ways, him to the house, me to play in the fields with my dog Rusty.

It was years before I realized we were thinking the same thoughts about snow and poverty, not understanding why some people did other people wrong when there was nothing to gain from it.

Mother kept us from getting too morose with her baking. When we got too down from too much thinking, she set to baking and brought us out of it with her cakes and pies, donuts and jelly rolls. These days, people would say it was a sugar rush that brought us out of those funks. I say it was love. Pure love. A mother and a wife's love.

*

Everyone in town said Old Add was a foundling. They said the old folks that raised him found him on their doorstep. They didn't ask anybody about a lost baby, they just took him in and kept him, like it was nobody's business, like he didn't have a mother or father anywhere that might want their baby boy back. Anyway, nobody ever showed up in Cross Grove asking about a baby, so they got to keep him just like they'd known all along they would.

People said those old folks were a mean, dry pair. They attended the Methodist church every Sunday, just like my family always has. They never spoke to anybody. They kept to themselves out on their old farm and didn't seem to have any other kin. As far as the townspeople knew, that baby was the only human who ever showed up out there. And I bet that baby only stayed with them because there was no other choice.

Old Add caused me personal trouble. You see, once or twice a year he came to our farm, made us a surprise visit, and stayed for a week or two. My pals from town teased me about it, and that made me mad. Nobody ever knew when he was going to show up or leave. He'd done it ever since I could remember. He never visited anyone else's place, just ours. Other than that, he stayed out on that old farm of his.

Old Add showed up, followed Dad around, and never said a word. I never heard him speak. I couldn't talk to Dad like I usually did when Old Add was around. Dad said I should keep quiet and respect Old Add's ways. It was quite irritating if you were like me, full of plenty to say, and wanting somebody to listen real close and maybe admire your words.

Besides that, Old Add liked Mother's cooking too much to suit me. He just about ate us out of house and home on every visit. When he showed up, I knew there wasn't going to be any leftover pie for me until after he was gone.

Old Add had another peculiar habit besides his need for visiting us. Every time I saw him, he was holding three large bird books clutched tight to his chest, like a shield of some kind. I did some mighty pondering over it now and then. I reckon he must have been afraid somebody might try to take those books away from him. I wondered where he got the books from and what they meant to him, but nobody would tell me anything. Once when he was visiting us, I came right out and asked him about them danged old bird books.

"Where'd you get those bird books?"

He didn't look at me or answer, but Dad shook his head no at me. He was wearing that strong look on him I didn't see very often. I shut my mouth right then, got myself right up from my chair and left. After that, I didn't dare ask that old man anything.

"Old Add ain't much of a talker." That's what the old timers hanging around the general store said about him before they snickered. They said that was called a dry joke when I asked them what they meant. They were the only ones who could tell a body who Old Add was and what he had done. I watched them treat him with grim respect and keep their distance from him. It seemed to me that anybody knowing anything about him was so old they'd lost their memory when it came to talking about him. They wouldn't tell a body much of anything at all.

Maybe it was because there was something about him that kind of dried you up and slowed you down when he was around. Or maybe it was the haunted look in his black eyes, like something wild and cold and untamed lived in there.

*

I turned thirteen and took up following Dad around, for I planned on being just like him and I needed to know exactly how to do it. He said he didn't know from one minute to the next whether I was going to call him Dad, Father, Tex, Roy, or St. Pete.

I was getting taller. Everybody said I was plumb full of questions and that's why I was getting so big. But that was how I learned things. I wasn't going to give up the habit of asking, even though it was a lot of work to keep it up. I worked hard to make a practice of asking questions about things I never cared about, or even thought about before. Dad said he thought I might grow up to be a lawyer.

"I just might!" I told him.

I worried all my questions like a dog gnawing a bone until I figured out whether they were good ones before I asked them. I know it took me long enough to think some of them up!

I kept my questions away from Mother though, 'cause she wouldn't answer a single one. Instead, she stayed after me for swiping pieces of her cakes and pies and meat and running off with them. Worse, she wanted to cut my hair for me all the time.

Then Old Add showed up at our place again, and I knew I'd have to go without extra sweets for a couple of weeks, but my hair would most likely be safe, for Mother would be busy cooking for him.

Old Add wasn't much for setting in a chair. He just stood around. He ate standing up, too. He ate what Mother handed him. She always piled his plate higher than anybody else's, even though he wouldn't set at the table with us.

Mother took his plate from him when it was bare and filled it as many times as he emptied it. She heaped a plate with dessert for him, and she wrapped up cookies for him to carry around in his pockets.

When Old Add wasn't eating, he just stood around some more and stared at us while his long bony fingers worried the edges of his old bird books. Dad fixed him a pallet on bales of hay out in the barn, winter and summer, for he wouldn't sleep in the house like regular folks. Of course, our barn was pretty snug, so Dad didn't worry too much about putting bedding out there for him in the winter.

When Old Add got ready to leave our place, he left without a goodbye to anybody. After he left, Mother and Dad acted like he was never there. They went out of their way to not speak his name or say one word about his visit. It was all very puzzling to me.

It was still winter and freezing cold when Old Add left a few days later. I asked Dad if he'd given him a ride somewhere, but he shook his head no.

"He left before I could make the offer," Dad answered.

I figured I was old enough now to be told more about Old Add, so I trailed Dad out to the barn to help feed the livestock. When the chores were done, I set down on a bale of hay and rested my back up against the barn wall and studied Dad.

People said I looked just like him, and I wanted to remember what I would look like when I got old. He was husky in his old plaid farm jacket. His straight, straw-colored hair poked out from under his brown fur cap. His eyes were light blue above a straight nose above a wide mouth and square chin. His features were woven together with fine lines and deep wrinkles. He had what the farmers around here called a weathered look. I didn't have any of that look yet, but I liked it, and I sometimes wondered what held my face together or anybody else's that didn't have that weathered look. After a while, I spoke real casual like,

"What about Old Add?"

Dad spoke kind of sharp back at me, "First of all, his name isn't Old Add."

"Well, that's what everybody calls him behind his back!" I said defensively. Before he could call me down again, I said, "You all act funny around him."

Dad sat down on the bale across from me. The barn was warm, comforting with cattle smells and the sounds they made munching the hay and grain in their stalls. The wind was blowing harder outside. I sniffed the air. New snow was coming. The smell of it was sweet on the air. There were no drafts inside our solid wood barn. Dad and the neighbors rebuilt it from the old, falling down barn that once stood in its place. That was back when Dad took over the farm.

Dad came from good German farm stock that pioneered their way to the state of Illinois, into the big city of Chicago. Dad worked hard, saved his money and bought this farm. My uncles and aunts and grandparents all lived in Chicago. Sometimes they came to visit and brought cloth and things for mother and tools and other things from their general store for Dad.

All of them were overloaded with common sense and physical strength. They were practical to a fault, dry natured, and not very wordy. They said I was more like Mother's family, wordy and curious about the world. I wondered how I would turn out, since we shielded my little Mother from most things. She was busy and bright, but frail, like a little wren. I was taller than her for the past two years. Dad protected her from any cruelties or meanness he suspected might take place. I learned from him and followed suit.

"Well, Son," Dad sighed, "I guess I can answer part of your questions, 'cause I know you won't stop 'til I do. But you need to keep in mind that a man never really knows everything about another man. There's a part of everybody that's their own business to take care of, a part they never tell anyone else about. It's supposed to be that way. Everyone has a place in them too deep to figure out easy. Sometimes, when a person gets old enough, they figure out part of it before they die. Nobody ever understands it all. Right now, you are seeing the world through a child's eyes."

He gave me a long, blue look as if considering whether to go on talking or not, or whether he'd used up enough words for the time being. I stared back at him earnestly, like I was the best boy he'd ever seen. That must have caused him to finally go on with his story.

He said, "What you're asking about is a story that started out with strong roots steeped in hate. There are different kinds of hates, just like there are different kinds of loves. Addition Jones' story has got a bunch of different kinds of hates and loves mixed up in it.

"You remember how we always called my dad Pops?" he asked. I nodded. When I was a child, I wasn't able to pronounce "grandfather" or any form of the word, so grandpa told me to call him Pops". The name stuck long after he passed away.

"Well, Pops gave Addition Jones the bird books he carries around. They were friends when they were young men. He told me what I know about Addition Jones."

I stared at Dad, my mouth hanging open in astonishment. He ignored my look.

"Remember hearing about the old folks that raised Addition Jones? Their names were Hester and Abraham Smith. People didn't know there was a child out on the Smith farm until Hester Smith came in town to get medicine to treat the boy when he was bad sick and about to die. Doc James asked her who the medicine was for. She didn't want to tell him, but he wouldn't give it to her until she told.

He was thunderstruck when she said it was for a boy they were keeping. He asked her how old the boy was. She told him it was none of his business. He asked her why nobody had ever seen him and was he old enough to go to school. She told him she was raisin' the boy for one of her kin. She said they were raising him to be a farm hand, so he didn't need to go to school. Then she told him to mind his own business again.

Doc James let it go, and gave her the medicine, but he wondered if she was telling the truth. You see, he remembered a baby disappearing two counties over a few years back. Somebody stole a baby boy, and there was a big ruckus over it. We heard the baby's mother went crazy from the loss, and her man wasn't far behind her. But the people over there didn't do much about the kidnapping because the man and woman that lost the baby were Gypsies, and they believed Gypsies were heathens because they didn't go to regular churches.

The law chose to assume another Gypsy stole the baby from them, although they never said it. The search was half-hearted. It didn't go on very long, and they never found the baby.

Doc James rode out to the Smith farm to check on the boy. He stopped on the hill overlooking their house and watched a boy moving bales of hay out by the barn. He watched the boy a few minutes, then decided that even though he looked like a Gypsy, he was way too big to be the age the stolen baby would have been. So, he left it alone too."

Dad studied me for a minute before saying, "People lived in a different time back then. They didn't think the way we do now. But some wrongs are always wrong, no matter when they happen. Those kinds of wrongs aren't about religion. They are about the bigger, never-ending battle between Good and Evil that's always going on. I guess that fight will go on as long as humans live on Earth. Son, if you ever see something you think might be wrong in your lifetime, I hope you'll try to do something to right it, not look the other way like those people did."

I frowned at him in puzzlement. He was trying to make me feel different about Old Add, I just knew it. I was on to his tricks!

I asked him, "What do you mean?"

He hardly ever spoke like this to me. He ignored my question and went on with his story.

"Back then, the Census taker was authorized to pay a cash dollar to everybody giving him an extra name to put on his list. I guess the old people raising him wanted that dollar. But they didn't give his last name as theirs. Instead, they wrote down Addition Jones, nephew, as a mean joke. What a ridiculous, cruel name to give someone!

Pops said those old folks worked Addition Jones day and night out on that old farm. They never let him go off the place. They made him call them Mr. Smith and Mrs. Smith. He slept out in the barn and rarely was allowed in the house. Hester Smith handed him his food through the screen door just as soon as he was big enough to live outside, like he was an animal or a dog she was feeding. He carried the food out to the barn or stood on the porch to eat, didn't matter what the weather was.

They raised him and worked him hard, and kept him out of their way. The worst sin that happened was nobody stopped them. He never got to meet anybody else. I guess everybody forgot he was a human being."

Dad watched my reaction to his words with the look in his eyes he got when he felt real strong about something. I stared back at him solemnly. I didn't like thinking about Old Add the way he was talking. Dad was expecting me to be a man in a way I didn't know about yet. I don't know what I was expecting to hear about Old Add, but it sure wasn't this! All I felt was a passing sadness for a lost boy I'd never met. Dad went on with his story.

"The Smiths attended the same Methodist church we do. They showed up early every Sunday morning, stood apart outside with their hands folded, their faces closed tight until the church doors opened. Neither one spoke to the rest of us. They gave a polite, grim little hello to the preacher now and then. They never sang the church songs or tithed.

People knew by then there was a boy out on their farm, and they knew how mean those old people were, but they didn't ask any questions. They ignored the boy's plight. People did that back then, before there were laws preventing ownership of lost or captured people.

Hester Smith always wore a white apron covering the same black dress every Sunday. She wore black lace-up shoes and kept her gray hair screwed up in a tight little knot on the top of her head. Abraham Smith wore an old black suit and a knob hat smelling like mothballs. In the winter, the two of them rode to church in an old two-seater sleigh."

Dad settled back further on the hay bale. I picked out a fat piece of hay stem and started chewing on it.

"Your grandfather happened to be close in age to Addition Jones. Pops kept hearing the rumors about the ghost boy living out on the old Smith farm. People wanted him to be a ghost, but he wasn't."

Dad grinned at me, his light blue eyes twinkling. He liked remembering his father because he liked him. I guess that runs in our family, for I like Dad very much, too.

"Your grandfather never met a stranger. He never missed out on knowing anybody living in this territory. Pops liked people. There's not many of the older ones he knew left around here now. He knew everybody's habits, too. He knew who made the best pie, and when to be there for it, kind of like you do."

I nodded vigorously. There was nothing better than cherry pie!

"Well, the stories and rumors about the boy out on the farm kept growing. Pop's curious nature pushed on him hard to find out if the rumors were true. He didn't like the stories of a boy being isolated out on the old farm at the mercy of the Smiths, and nobody doing anything about it. But nobody else seemed to think anything was wrong with it, so he kept quiet.

Pops set in church every Sunday, wondering and watching the Smiths come and go every week without a word being said about the boy's whereabouts. Why wasn't the boy in church, too?

The time came when he couldn't stand his confusion over the right and wrong of it any longer. He became determined to find out for himself what was going on out there."

Dad's voice sharpened. "One more thing before I tell you any more. That man you see is just a shell of his former self. He was a hell of a fierce, strong man before his mind shortened. His mind isn't clear any more. It don't work right. Nowadays, his only memories are of being a lost boy and my father's friend."

I gave him a long look. I would never tease Old Add again to impress the other boys.

Dad went on with his story.

Chapter 2. The Ghost Boy

Fractions
Actions

"Winter set in. Pops made his plan. All of a sudden he took up bird watching. He ordered bird books and pored over them in front of the family. Then he pretended to go out hunting for a rare kind of winter bird that only lived around here. Instead of going to church with his folks and the family on Sundays, he made up a big whopper about finding that rare bird so he could get out of going, for it was the only time the Smiths would be gone from the farm and couldn't run him off their place.

He hunted for that bird every night after school and on weekends until people got used to him missing church most Sundays.

One Saturday night, a deep snow fell. The next morning, Pops went out bird hunting. He set out on his snowshoes with a pair of short skis strapped across his back. He took all the shortcuts he'd tested, and traveled the back way across the fields until he reached the Smith farm. He hid out behind a cluster of trees up on the knoll overlooking their farm and waited. Pretty soon, he saw a large young man about his own age hitch up horses to the little sleigh the Smiths rode to church in.

Pops hid behind the trees until the Smiths got in the sleigh and drove off. He watched them until they were out of sight. Then he looked at the yard, but the young man was gone. "

Dad settled back to relate the crux of the story, a thing he'd done only a handful of times before.

"Pops carried an old fob watch his grandpa gave him. He took the watch out and checked the time. He figured it would be at least two hours before the Smiths started home from church. He took off his snowshoes, put on his skis, started whistling, and slid down the hill, right smack dab into the middle of the yard. Nothing moved on the place. It stayed silent as a tomb.

He took off his skis, went up to the front door of the house and knocked loud. He figured the boy was inside because it was pretty cold outside. He waited, but nobody answered, so he walked back out in the middle of the yard and called Addition Jones name.

Nothing. He waited a little bit before he wandered over to the barn and opened the door. By then he realized Addition Jones wasn't going to show himself. He wanted to give it one more try though, before he gave up and went home empty-handed.

He went in the barn, closed the door, set down on a bale of hay, pulled out that little harmonica he carried, and started playing. He heard a door open behind him, but he kept on playing like he never heard a thing.

Addition Jones stepped around the corner and stood there, watching him. Pops kept on playing while they looked each other over. The boy was a tall, big boned kid with swarthy skin, black hair, and eyes as black as midnight coals. He wore a pair of homemade, dirty coveralls, a ragged coat, and big sloppy barn boots. He was taller than Pops and heavier boned.

Well, Pops stopped playing and introduced himself and tried to shake hands with him, but the boy wouldn't do it. Pops figured maybe he didn't know what a handshake was.

"You're Addition Jones?" he asked.

The boy nodded. Pops reached into his coat pocket, pulled out the bag of cookies he'd stole from the kitchen and laid them down on a bale of hay. The boy worked his way over to the cookies and grabbed them."

Dad reached over and ruffled my hair. He said, "That wouldn't do for you, would it, boy?"

"It sure wouldn't!" I answered with heartfelt sincerity.

I was in another growth spurt and everybody teased me about having two hollow legs that couldn't be filled up.

"I even eat Aunt Jenny's cooking when there's nothing else around," I said.

Dad chuckled and said she probably appreciated me a lot these days, before he went on with his story.

"Pops offered Addition Jones the harmonica. He took it and tried to play. Pops showed him his antique watch and let him hold it. The boy listened to the watch ticking, looked at the hands moving on the face, and gave it back to him. He motioned for Pops to follow him to the back of the barn.

He led the way to a crude door covering a rectangle cut in the barn wall. The makeshift door led into a little homemade lean-to with plank walls and a ceiling made of scrap lumber. Dried mud and straw was packed between the boards of the walls and ceiling for insulation. Boards covered the bare earth floor. A small wood burning stove with a metal pipe running up through the ceiling set in the middle of the floor. The rusty little stove squatted on a sheet of old scrap metal. A narrow, metal framed army cot with a couple of faded quilts on it was pulled close to the stove.

"Is this where you live?" Pops asked. The boy nodded.

"All the time?" The boy nodded again.

"Pops was shocked. He didn't know what to say. Both boys moved to the stove to warm their hands. Pops said the boy finally started talking. Just before time for church to let out, Pops gave him the harmonica and told him to take it to the fields to play so the Smith's wouldn't hear it. Then they went outside and brushed away all his signs so the Smith's would never know he'd been there.

Well, Pops started sneaking over there every Sunday instead of attending church. He told everybody he was still out hunting that dang rare bird. It was during that time he sent away for the three bird books Addition Jones carries. Pops gave him his short skis, taught him to use them, and told him to keep them out of sight of the old folks. At home, Pops told everyone he'd busted his skis. Before long, he had a new pair."

Dad waited for the answer to the bird book question to sink in. I nodded. Yep. That answered the eternal bird book question for me! I sighed. This sure was a burdensome, sad story!

"Pops stole chalk, a slate board and pencils, and other stuff from the schoolhouse and carried it out to the farm. He taught Addition Jones to read and cipher numbers better. The old folks had taught him to read the Bible and count just good enough to behave and work for them. In return, Addition Jones showed him how he stacked the bales of straw against the outside of the little lean-to. The bales kept his room warm in the winter and cool in the summer. He showed him the cords of wood he chopped to heat the house and the lean-to for the winter.

He introduced Pops to the wild animals living in the fence rows and the other wild places on the farm. He taught him how to call wild turkeys and how to make the sounds of squirrels and birds. He taught Pops things nobody else thought about learning from nature."

Dad was some kind of proud himself when he said, "I learned some of it from Pops, and Addition Jones knows that. He has no children, and he might be proud of me for learning some of what he taught Pops. I'll probably never know, but I suspect that's the reason he visits us."

Dad fixed me with a glint in his eyes. "When you're older and your thinking has matured, I might pass some of what I learned from him on to you."

I stared at him, dumbfounded.

"Why do I have to wait?"

He ignored my question, as usual. After taking my measure with stern eyes, he went on with his story.

"Pops told Addition Jones about the rare bird he was supposed to be out searching for, and when the new bird books he ordered came in, he gave them to Addition Jones. He received them as a treasure and hid them under a floorboard in his little room. He read them from cover to cover, over and over again."

*

"Well, Pops was too young to understand the seriousness of his friendship with Addition Jones. He started going back to church with his folks, for there was a pretty girl he wanted to impress, instead of visiting Addition Jones."

Dad reached across the bale of hay and tapped me on the arm. "That pretty girl was your grandmother, and if he wanted her to be his girl, he had to go to church on Sundays."

I studied him. "Just like you," I said. He grinned and nodded.

"Yep," he said.

"But Pops wanted both. He wanted Addition Jones as a friend and your grandmother as a wife. The solution seemed simple to him. Why, he would just bring Addition Jones into town and introduce him around. Folks would take to him, and something good would work out. Maybe he could leave that old farm, and work for money for somebody else and get his own place. Maybe he could rent over at the boardinghouse and make friends with people.

Pops persuaded Addition Jones to sneak off the farm and go into town with him. The Smiths would never find out, for they only went to town when they had to. The two boys went all over town and looked at everything. Pops took him into all of the stores and introduced him to everybody. But Pops didn't know the amount of guilt the people in town had stored up over not righting the wrong sitting on their doorstep for years. Pops paraded that wrong right in front of their faces, and introduced them to it.

It was obvious the boy they were seeing had suffered. Wild looking, unkempt and awkward, with few social skills, he stayed close to Pops and was short spoken and abrupt with everyone he met. No one saw his hands and mouth shaking except Pops. Pops didn't know what was wrong. He didn't understand why nobody smiled when he introduced Addition Jones to them.

They went to town a few more times together. Each time it was an ordeal for both of them. Pops didn't know what else to do, so he left Addition Jones on his own. Pops was in love, and his mind was on his girl. He was too young to understand what it meant to Addition Jones when he stopped coming around.

Pops started spending his extra time with your grandmother. He felt bad over not going to see Addition Jones anymore, so he went out to the farm to explain to him that he had a girlfriend now and he would be too busy with her to visit much. He advised him to leave the farm, move to town, and get out in the world.

The next Sunday, Addition Jones showed up at church. That was the first time the old folks knew anything. He sent them off to church in the sleigh, and pretty soon he came trotting in behind them. The Smiths were mad about it, but they didn't say anything in front of anybody.

Everybody in the church kept turning their heads and staring at him. Pops said he was quite a sight in his barn boots and homemade, ill-fitting clothes hanging like rags off of him. The children whispered. The Scarecrow was in church! They didn't know whether to be afraid or make fun of him.

After church, the Smiths climbed in their buggy and drove away. They acted like they never seen him at all. Nobody knew what happened when he got home, but he showed up to church every Sunday after that. He came on foot by himself. He washed and mended his own clothes, and they were always too short legged and short sleeved for him. He cut his own hair. It stood up in straight, black hanks around his head. After a while, some of the church people started getting used to him. The barber in town cut his hair and smoothed it out. The preacher gave him a Bible.

One Sunday after church, old man Smith tried to take the buggy whip to him, but he grabbed it away from the old man, broke it and threw it on the ground. That same Sunday, he told Pops the old woman would hardly feed him anymore. He was forced to go in the house where he wasn't welcome and take food from the kitchen to survive. They wouldn't lock him out though, because they needed him to work the place. If they locked him out, he'd leave, and they knew it. Pops mentioned his bad situation to your grandmother, and the church ladies started fixing him up a food package to carry home every Sunday.

Everything settled down after that. Pops got in the habit of walking him part of the way home after church. He left him to go on by himself at the fork in the road leading to your grandmother's house.

Addition Jones didn't know how people were supposed to act. He came to everything late. So he decided he would like your grandmother too. He started leaving little whittled animals and such on her porch. He wouldn't speak to her because he was so bashful, but he watched her every Sunday in church. Pops didn't know what to think of it, but he was awfully good-natured, and your grandmother told him to not make too much of it, that Addition would get over it in time.

Then one Sunday, he walked right down to the front of the church and sat down beside your grandmother. Pops was setting on the other side of her. After church, your grandmother ordered Addition Jones not to set by her again. She told him your grandfather was her boyfriend, she didn't want anybody else. First he got embarrassed, then mad. He started setting in the back of the church and ignoring Pops and your grandmother.

Then he started following the preacher around, asking him all kinds of questions about the Bible. Now, the preacher was a good man. He passed the salt at the Sunday table just as quick as the next man. That means he put it away right good, son." Dad grinned at me.

"Addition Jones was growing up. The preacher became convinced he had a call to preach so he started taking him with him everywhere. Church attendance dropped off because nobody liked the preacher taking up with Addition Jones.

Well, things went on that way until the day he came running into town and said the Smiths had burned up in the old farmhouse. Everybody rushed out to their farm, but there wasn't much left to see. The house was burnt almost to the ground. It was a hot, quick burning fire. Nobody could search for bodies until the house cooled down.

Those old folks were misers, but they owned some of the richest bottom land in this county, and they owned a lot of it. They let most of it lay fallow and worked what little they needed to make a living.

They had plenty of money put away, but they weren't going to spend a dime of it on hired help when Addition Jones was there to do the farm work for them.

He said he was working in a back field and wasn't paying any attention to anything else. By the time he saw the smoke and ran home, the house was already up in blazes. He couldn't get inside and get them out, so he ran to town for help.

Pops said he fell apart. Somebody brought him a chunk of wood to set down on. Pops said he kept staring at his hands and shaking his head like he couldn't believe it. He put his head down in his hands and just set there. Nobody could get him to speak.

Somebody called in the county people, and they said nobody was supposed to touch anything until they got there. Cody Watson was the head of that bunch and the sheriff of this county back then. The preacher tried to take Addition Jones out of there, but he wouldn't go.

In a few days they sifted around and found the bones of the old folks and got them buried. Addition Jones slept in his little room out in the barn and watched everything they did every minute.

Well, Cody, he never said much, he just stood around and watched the rest of them work. He looked at a lot of things, and he looked a lot at Addition Jones, too. Then they held an inquest, and Cody dropped his bomb. He said he knew Addition Jones burnt the old folks up in that house, but he couldn't prove it, so Jones would get off scot free. Everybody in town was there and heard what Cody said.

Addition Jones seemed to think the people in town would still treat him the same way they did before the fire. But after what Cody said, folks believed he was guilty and took to avoiding him even more.

They finally had the perfect excuse not to listen to the child they abandoned to the Smiths or hear about his years of hardship with them. It was much easier to salve their conscience by believing he murdered the problem they'd ignored."

Dad fell quiet a minute before he went on with the tale.

"The preacher got him a lawyer who helped him get the Smiths' money and all of their fine land. He farmed a little bit of it and traded around here and there to get by on. But he had a hard time of it after he caught on that everybody believed he burned up the old folks in the house on purpose.

He stayed mad at everybody and they grew to openly hate him in return. About a year after the fire, he left Cross Grove. Nobody ever knew where he went or heard from him again. Before he left, he carried the bird books back to Pops and tried to give them to him. But Pops refused, and he was forced to keep them.

After he left, Pops went out to the old homestead to look it over. The empty barn, stable, and smaller buildings were padlocked shut. The old house lay in charred ruins. The fields were never plowed again. Over time, the weeds grew up, and nobody ever went near that old place. The townspeople were glad he was gone. With him gone, they were free to hate him and spread stories about him being a murderer.

Quite a few years went by before he came back. By that time, your grandfather and your grandmother were married. I was already born, as well as your Aunt Jenny and Uncle Henry.

After a while, it was set like stone in everybody's mind in Cross Grove that Addition Jones had murdered the Smiths. Nobody questioned it at all. It was a part of the town's history. Then Nell Miller showed up, and everything changed."

*

The barn door opened. Mother stepped inside and shut the door behind her. A few snowflakes whirled in with her and settled on her soft brown hair. I studied her for a minute and thought she looked like a beautiful, soft, brown and gray barn dove. She smiled at us and said, "I've got hot coffee and pie waiting for you up at the house."

I looked at Dad. An unspoken agreement to leave off with the story passed between us. I think we were both relieved. He'd given me enough to think about for a long time. I figured I could wait on the rest of Addition Jones's story until another day.

Chapter 3. Fate Comes Calling

Renditions
Conditions

At noon on a hot summer day in the year of 1895, a small black buggy made its way slowly down the dusty main street of the small farming town of Cross Grove, Illinois. The buggy came to a stop in front of Webster's general store. A tall, thin woman stepped out of the buggy, shook her skirts into place, and began climbing the steps to the wide plank sidewalk running the length of Main Street. She stopped and looked in the window of the general store before she opened the door and stepped inside. She stood still, calmly waiting until her eyes adjusted to the dim interior.

Barrels of pickles and other goods were lined up in a long row beneath the wide wood service counter. The wall behind the counter held shelves of neatly stacked bolts of cloth and more. Shiny glass candy jars filled with a rainbow of colors were lined up on a long table in the front window.

The woman peered towards the back of the store. In the dim light, she saw a squat black stove with silver foot rails, and a bunch of old men sitting around a wood barrel with a checkerboard on its top. They were arguing with each other.

She shifted nervously from foot to foot, standing there for what seemed to her an eternity before the old men noticed her. They fell silent, stared at her and waited. She moved cautiously towards them down the length of the room. In a low voice, she asked,

"Can anybody tell me where Addition Jones lives?"

The old men didn't answer. She felt them draw back from her before the waves of hostility hit her. The old men were glaring at her. She felt faint for a moment. Then she sighed. She didn't know why this was happening, but she was too damn far beyond tired to care. She stared back at them and waited. Somebody knew something, regardless of their unexplained hostility.

The old men looked her over, glanced at each other, and shrugged. They couldn't guess her age. She looked both young and old. She was rangy, spare boned, and tall, too tall for a woman, close to six foot. A woman should be smaller than her man. They shook their heads at each other, certain without even a small wager that she was a spinster.

The woman's eyes were the same slate gray as the serviceable, ankle length dress she wore. Her eyes looked like they'd been washed a thousand times and mended just about as much as her dress. Her narrow, long black shoes were dusty with travel. Her fine, straight blond and mostly gray hair was screwed up in a tight little knot on top of her head.

She bore their stares calmly. The only sound in the store was the big, round clock high on the wall behind the front counter, ticking time away in measured beats. A door opened at the back of the store. The sound broke the silence. A man strolled behind the counter. The woman turned to him.

"I need to know where Addition Jones lives."

He stared at her, speechless, just like the other men.

Another one! she thought. She didn't know what was going on, and she didn't care. She was determined to find out what she needed to know. Patiently she watched him until he got his bearings.

"What do you want with him?" the man asked.

"I've got to see him and tell him something real important," she answered.

The man studied the tall, thin reed of a woman swaying before him. She looked as worn out as a person could be and still be standing. He cleared his throat.

"My name is Claude Webster. I own this store. It's a surprise to have anybody ask about Addition Jones. He doesn't live here anymore, and nobody knows where he went. We haven't seen him around here in years."

He watched the hope drain out of her. Her face went white. She swayed forward, clasped her hands together, and looked down at them. He ran and grabbed a rocking chair from the back of the store, carried it to her and guided her down into it. She sank down into it like the wind had gone out of her sails. He hurried behind the counter, poured a mug of hot coffee and carried it to her. She sipped the mug of coffee with shaking hands and ignored the old men edging closer and closer.

As soon as Claude saw she was going to take the coffee okay, he dipped a couple pickled eggs out of a jar, sliced them, and spread them out on a thick slab of the homemade bread his wife Margaret had made. He folded the bread in half and carried the sandwich to her. She ate it in a few bites. In a couple minutes, her color came back. She lifted her head and gazed at the old men gathered around her. Then she gazed at Claude in despair.

"I guess it's hopeless to try and find him. Did he grow up here, like I heard?"

The old men nodded at her.

"And he's never coming back?"

They nodded again.

"Are you sure?"

They nodded again.

She took a deep breath and stared at them like she was making a decision about something.

"I've got to tell somebody.... Since this is where he lived, maybe I'll just tell it now, so it gets witnessed in the place where he lived. Maybe it will make things right somehow. Then I can go back home and start over. That is, if you don't mind. I just want to get this over with," she said in a weary voice.

Claude studied her. She didn't seem to realize she was sitting in a general store open for business. He looked at the old men. They nodded at him as if they'd read his mind. They were acting casual, hovering close to her, not too close, just close enough to hear every word. He went to the front door and turned the key in the lock. He flipped over the closed sign so it showed out the front window. Then he came back, pulled up a chair, and sat down facing her. Relief swept over her face when he nodded at her.

"May as well tell it," Claude said.

She took a deep breath and began her story.

*

"My father's name was Grady Miller, and I'm Nell Miller." She spoke carefully, ruminating over the beginning words, testing them. "My father loved the drink. He was a handsome man, not plain like me. He had an ugly temper," she sighed.

"I'm gonna' start at the beginning if you don't mind."

They nodded. Her voice smoothed out. She began speaking as though she was reciting pages out of a book.

"My folks married young. Then I was born. There weren't anymore because of Mother's trouble having me. Her father, my grandfather, gave us the little farm I grew up on. He paid the taxes on it. It was all rock and thin soil. His own place wasn't much better.

Like I said, my father was a handsome man, a charmer. He kept a good horse and fine clothes for himself. His smile could light up the sun, but he had a mile long streak of mean pride. His temper was high, and he wasn't one you wanted to make mad at you, for he would find a way to make you pay for it if he could.

Mother and I worked the farm while my father drank and came and went as he pleased. Sometimes we didn't see him for days, but we knew better than to ask him where he went. He kept us out in the country and away from other folks. We worked hard and made the place better than it was before. Then Mother passed away."

Nell turned her head away from them for a minute.

"I didn't get much schooling, and there wasn't anyone else to turn to after she died. Besides, I was always too busy with the chickens and the garden and the cows to even think about meeting other people. I was used to being alone. I didn't see any other choice. I didn't have a dime to my name, and I didn't know anybody, so I stayed right there and worked the place while he ran around. I doubt if he noticed my mother's passing since I was still there to work the place. He just kept right on with his drinking and other bad habits."

She glanced at Claude and looked away. The clock ticked loudly in the silence.

"Not long ago, he took sick and stayed laid up in bed. He couldn't run off like always. He kept getting worse, and I finally got Doc Williams from town to come out and look at him. The doctor told him, right in front of me, that he didn't have much time left, and he better mend his fences quick. It was plain the doctor didn't like him. A couple of days later, he tried to burn the house down. He managed to burn part of the living room before I saw the smoke and put it out. I moved us out to the barn until I could get the house back in shape.

Maybe his conscience got to bothering him. I'll never know. I never knew him to say a good word about anybody, but a little while before he died, he told me about something bad he done a long time ago... that's the reason I'm here."

She huffed out a breath and looked down at her hands.

"He said that not long after he married my mother, when he was off on one of his drinking sprees, he met a young woman. He said he fell in love with her, and she was all he could think about. He lied to her and told her he was a single man, and he made trip after trip to see her.

He planned to leave my mother and take up with her, but he started drinking too much and showed his temper in front of her, and it scared her. She asked around about him and found out he was a married man. He said she slipped around real quick behind his back and married another man to get away from him.

He said he couldn't get her off his mind, that she was his, so he rode over to her and her new man's house. He hid on the hill above their house and watched them. He said her man was a dark feller; he didn't like the looks of him, but she seemed pretty happy with him. He said it didn't take long before all he could think about was getting back at her for doing him wrong. He kept watching them, trying to figure out what to do to pay her back. Then the woman and her man had a baby, and he seen the way to do it.

One day, the woman was hanging out clothes. The baby was sleeping in a basket under a tree by the clothesline. She went back in the house to get something, and he slipped down the hill and stole the sleeping baby and a sheet out of the basket. He fixed the covers so it looked like the baby was still in the basket, and ran back up the hill.

The baby didn't make a sound. He said he thought about leaving it on the ground, but changed his mind. He tied it to himself with the sheet, got on his horse and slipped away from their place. He said he rode the rest of the day and half the night. He couldn't seem to stop.

Finally, he came to a farmhouse, slipped up on the porch, and laid the baby up against the front door. The baby was still wrapped up in the sheet. He never even looked at it. Then he got back on his horse and rode home. He thought on his death bed that what he did was funny, that she deserved it."

Nell scrubbed her hand across her mouth like she'd tasted something bad.

"But that wasn't all he done."

Claude looked at the old men gathered around them. A pin could have dropped in the store and they would have heard it fall. It was the first time he'd ever seen all of them quiet at the same time.

"He kept on slipping back over to the woman's house to watch her and her man, to see how bad he hurt them. The woman was never the same after he stole the baby from her. She wouldn't talk to anybody. She set in the yard or in the house by the window, staring down the road. He said he went right up to her one time and looked at her through the window, but she never gave any sign she saw him.

I don't know how many years he rode over there before he decided he'd forgive her and take her baby back to her. The idea worked on him, and he searched for a long time before he found the farm where he left the baby.

He planned to take the baby back, and nobody would catch him. But time doesn't stand still. The baby was now a large, strapping young boy. His plan had been foiled by time. He couldn't kidnap the baby again and take it back to the woman he wronged. He always carried whiskey with him. So he got mad, then he got drunk and set the house on fire where he left the baby, and rode home."

Nell looked at Claude and the old men. They were staring at her in shock. She took another deep breath.

"I was holding my father up so he could tell it to me. The last words he spoke in this world was Addition Jones. He said that's what they named the baby he stole. Then he died."

She shrugged, without a speck of grief but with the burden of unwanted restitution.

"So, I vowed to find Addition Jones, and tell him what my father did to him. This is the last thing I have to do before I leave that old farm. I don't know where I'll go or what I'll do, for I have no one. No relatives, not a friend in this world. But at last, in the telling of his black deeds, I breathe free of that evil excuse for a father!"

Her words fell into a deep well of astounded silence holding only the loud ticking clock behind the counter, a sound usually heard only in the midnight hours in the store.

Her head drooped. There was more to her story than she'd told them, but that part was none of their business. It was true Addition Jones' name was flung into her life with her father's last cruel words. She knew Grady Miller devised to saddle her with his guilt, using his last words. He wanted to keep her hurting and alone the rest of her life.

What he didn't know, and would never know, please God, was that he had gifted her with a companion. She was worried about losing him, evil as he was, for there was no one else. Anybody was better than nothing. The only place she knew was the drab little farm. There were no family, no friends, nothing. She didn't know how to make her way in life, or how to find a new purpose for living.

When she found out he was dying, all she felt was relief. Then she slowly grew frightened at being left alone. She ticked off the nothings she would have left, one after the other, every day in an endless litany. No children. No husband. No mother. No father. No sisters. No brothers. No cousins. Red the Rooster had died. Curly the pig was pork chops and bacon.

Every day, the emptiness loomed closer, insistent on her nothingness, her non-existence without someone, until she worked almost around the clock to quell the slow build of panic.

She gave him only what was absolutely necessary and turned away from his pleading looks of hate and misery. He'd done enough to her and her beloved mother, or so she'd believed, until his dying confession.

With nothing left to lose and no one to turn to, she grabbed on to the name branded in the black fire of his filthy, dying confession. A name he'd thrown at her with the last bit of venom left in him before he died. Now there was someone else. Now she would survive.

After he was dead, she sat beside him for a long time, trembling with the mindlessness of extreme fatigue and relief, unaware of the summer rain when it started tapping gently on the barn roof, cleansing and washing away the old ashes and dust.

The life he put her mother and her through was over. There was nothing left. No more of his drinking, sneaking and lying; no more waiting on him hand and foot; no more hurt or pain or ignoring their neediness. He was gone.

She stood, covered him with a blanket, and walked out into the rain. She held out her arms, raised her face to the sky and mouthed the name Addition Jones to herself. What an odd, ridiculous name it was! She didn't care.

She sighed with relief. At the very last minute God had mercy on her and answered her prayers for someone, anyone. For the time being at least, she would not be lost, a nameless nothing, a never remembered spirit that once walked the earth, not mattering to God or any other human being. She had Addition Jones now. She had his name, silly though it was, and she had a purpose on this Earth once again.

She sniffed the wet, warm dirt smell of the Earth and grimly smiled to herself. She would find Addition Jones and tell him what her father did to him. They could hate him together. Maybe they would end up being companions, like a brother and sister. Oh, the time they might spend together! She stood in the gentle, warm rain a long time, letting it wash away her aloneness before she went to town to get the doctor and undertaker.

Chapter 4. Finding Friends

Law of Averages
Vital statistics

Nell stirred herself out of her musings and gazed at the men gathered closely around her. They stared at her with looks of mingled pity, dread, scorn and disbelief. Their stunned silence ticked on and on in time with the clock.

Claude watched the tired, dusty woman sitting perfectly still in the rocking chair. No one knew what to say. Nell was as gray as her dress once again. It looked to Claude like she'd used up her last grain of grit in the telling of her story.

"Miz Miller, nobody here knows where Addition Jones is. He's been gone from these parts for many years. He left here about a year after the old folks that raised him burned up in their farmhouse. We haven't seen or heard from him since."

Nell blanched and looked at him.

"Oh my God! I didn't know anyone burned up in the fire! My father didn't tell me that part!"

Claude said calmly, "Why don't I walk you over to my house so you can meet my wife. I know she would like to meet you, and have you rest for a little while."

Claude helped Nell up out of the rocker. She didn't resist him. He jerked his head at one of the old men.

"Lester, watch the store for me. Nell, one of these other gents can take your horse and buggy over to the stable for you."

She barely remembered leaving the store. A short time later, she found herself walking up wide wood steps and standing in a house. There was an impression of green plants in orderly rows, sheer white curtains shading long windows, and the smell of laundry dried in sunshine.

The bed smelled of sunshine, too. Before she dozed off, she remembered being embraced by a woman carrying the sound of kindness in her voice. The woman led her upstairs to a bedroom where she fell into a large bed smelling of fresh, ironed sheets. She closed her eyes and sank into an exhausted sleep.

It was dusk when she woke up. She sat up and looked around. The bedroom was large and pleasant. There were amber colored, wide plank floors, sheer white curtains at two long windows, and walls papered in pale green with a thin border of white flowers at the ceiling and above the baseboards. The full bed was strategically placed to give a sweeping view of the front yard through the two windows. The headboard and footboard were blond wood matching a simple dresser and vanity.

Nell smoothed her hair and dress and made her way down the stairs. She heard the deep rumble of Claude's voice and a lighter one as she crossed to the kitchen doorway. Claude looked up and gave her an easy grin, one she was to come to know and like. The tall, rangy blond woman sitting at the kitchen table across from him stood up and scrubbed her hands across her apron.

"I'm Margaret," she said briskly. Nell looked at her round, smooth face. Kindness and efficiency radiated from her.

"Why, she makes me think of myself," Nell thought and smiled.

"I'm Nell Miller." They shook hands.

"I expect you need to know where the outhouse is and to wash up a little bit. We'll wait the pie on you," Margaret said.

A few minutes later, Nell sat down to leftovers from supper. The big round white plate held golden corn pone, cream gravy, crisp roast pork, and green beans. Margaret and Claude made small talk while Nell ate. Then they passed her a wedge of lemon pie and refilled her coffee cup. At last Claude yawned. Margaret took her cue from him.

"Nell, I know you need to bathe and sort things out, but you can start that tomorrow.

Why don't you go on back to bed, and we'll see how you feel in the morning?"

Relief washed over her.

"Thank you."

She wouldn't have to answer questions just yet. She knew she couldn't handle another thing today. Morning would come, a new day would dawn, and she would worry about it then.

She climbed the stairs, slipped quietly into the bedroom and closed the door. She undressed down to her white slip and lay down in the serene darkness of the bedroom. She pulled the sweet, outdoor scented covers up to her chin.

Slowly, hesitant at first, a steady stream of tears began to pour from her eyes. Surprised, she couldn't remember the last time she'd cried. Broken hearts happened to people, and the ready tears of childhood that healed the hurts her father inflicted dried up years ago. She thought they were gone forever. Hot, bitter tears slid down her cheeks while thoughts she never allowed poured through her mind. She'd survived a vile, despicable, evil, hateful excuse for a father. One who kidnapped and murdered! She wept on and off until her tears dried up, until she could think straight again.

When her father flung the truth of the hateful legacy he hoped to leave behind at her in his final moments, his mean, careless confession finally broke the bondage of hate and power he held over her. Now there was someone else instead of him. They would be better than him. His hold on her through making her pity him was at last gone, and she recognized it for the sickness it was.

She thanked God he'd killed it by leaving no words of love or gratitude behind, just his curse, and his hope the poison of it would somehow kill her. Astounded and hurt, she'd watched the hopeful hate flare-up in his face. In that instant, she completely let go of any pity she felt for him and grabbed on to the nameless, faceless man he'd wronged with hope and relief.

Addition Jones. He was hers now. He'd been done wrong by her father, too. They were companions who never knew about each other's existence. Her whole life shifted in a split second. Most of her life, she'd had a companion, albeit unknown. She was awed. And suddenly made stronger.

For that unmet man, she'd made her father's sins public knowledge this very day. The last dregs of pity for her mother and father washed away with her tears.

Addition Jones was gone. Nobody knew where. Gone for many years. That part was over. Still, he would remain her companion. Her confession on his behalf over with, her obligation to him fulfilled, maybe tomorrow she could think about making plans for a new life for herself. She fell asleep with new hope ticking time away on the small, round-faced clock on the nightstand.

*

Margaret and Nell took to each other immediately. The two of them recognized how alike they were. They laughed at each new discovery. Though they'd lived different lives, they bore the same nature. Both in their late middle years, both childless, each one could have efficiently mothered many children. Each one would have competently handled every challenge motherhood brought. But there were no children, so their great need to organize, supervise, and do for someone else had carried them down different roads.

Nell turned to the old, neglected farm and the land. She stayed busy on the farm, taking care of her sick mother and wandering, lazy father. It was her sole purpose in life to do for all the things needing her. From early childhood, she milked cows, fed chickens and planted wildflowers in orderly rows around the front porch to bring her mother cheer. She kept the porch swept, the house clean, and did most of the cooking and sewing.

Nell's mother was fairly well-educated. She taught Nell to read and write and do her sums;

she instructed her homely daughter to have good manners and speak correctly. Nell formed the habit of reading her mother's Bible every evening so she wouldn't lose her reading skills.

Margaret went in a different direction. Her practical nature easily figured out what the results of things would be before she acted. Shortly after she and Claude were married, she insisted he carry a few things in the general store just for women. He resisted at first, but before he knew what happened, she baked him things that melted in his mouth and honeyed him into it. She'd taken over a small corner of the front window. "Just as an experiment!" she laughed merrily to him. She held up her hands cajolingly to Nell, laughing as she told the story.

In the beginning she displayed a few yards of rich, shockingly expensive fabric from back East in a corner of the window. Then she placed a set of delicate, expensive turquoise hair combs and two hand painted silk scarves against the expensive fabric.

The old men who played checkers in the back of the store grumbled about it. They thought Claude was silly to give in and put a bunch of worthless things in the general store window.

"The men won't come in here, 'cause it's gittin' too uppity for a plain farmer's town! You ain't been married very long, Claude."

The old man turned to the other old men for validation. They nodded vigorously.

"A new wife always turns your head, but it'll pass. Everybody knows farm women only want plain, common sense things."

Claude stayed mild with them.

"Well, we're gonna' give it a chance. She's a fine cook, you know."

The old men shook their heads and went back to playing checkers and spitting tobacco juice into spittoons, satisfied with their opinions until they watched their sons stroll into the store, red-faced and awkward, to buy the cloth and the set of combs and scarves out of the window for their women.

Soon the women were strolling in and out of the general store. Everything Margaret displayed in the window sold out quickly at a good profit. Claude was one who could read the handwriting on the wall. He helped Margaret place orders for more items to go in the window.

The wives of the old men playing checkers in the back of the store started coming to town to critique the window displays. They complained that the store didn't carry the special tatting threads and other old-fashioned things they needed. Claude quickly made up another order list to satisfy them.

Things were changing. There was no stopping it once it started. The old men began complaining about not having a place to get away from the women anymore. Some of the younger and more thoughtful farm men began to wonder why they didn't know their womenfolk craved pretty things.

The wives of the farmers in the little isolated farming town began blooming. They planned dinners and birthday parties and church suppers so they could show off their new finery to each other. Easier, kinder relationships began to offset the harsh reality of living a life filled with too much hard work, not enough time, and no place to go.

And once in a while, the husband of a plain farm woman began to understand what the beautiful, personal things he bought for his wife meant to her, and the ways they knew each other deepened. Claude laughed in appreciation when he realized what was happening.

He shook his head and said admiringly to Margaret, "I've got the most amazing, smartest wife anyone could ever hope to have. You've created a domino effect. Everything is getting better!"

*

At the end of their second day together, Margaret invited Nell to stay with them until she got her bearings. Nell agreed. She slept, ate, rested, and helped Margaret with the

53

housework. She began talking, healing from her isolation and loneliness. The two of them let the flow of their talk go where it would as the bond between them strengthened.

Nell talked more to Margaret than she'd talked to anyone in her whole life. Her words poured out like an un-damned river. Margaret listened to Nell describe her solitary life on the old farm with her sickly mother, alcoholic father, and the hard work. Each day, Nell's words emptied out, and a kind of peace took their place. Margaret gave her gentle examples of reluctant prisoners, mystical hermits, reclusive eccentrics, and other isolates that had survived different kinds of loneliness.

"Always for a higher purpose," Margaret stated firmly.

Nell told Margaret everything, except how she grabbed on to Addition Jones to survive having no one. In secret, she was grateful to him. His name had carried her to this place, where she met Margaret and Claude, her first friends. He was doing her a world of good, but it looked like he might never know it.

She listened avidly while Margaret told her what she knew of Addition Jones' history. In Nell's mind, she stood beside the isolated boy, then the young man who grew up on the old Smith farm, ventured into town and eventually ran away.

Both of them had been used as workhorses, unloved and untended, kept isolated from other people to work old farms. At least her mother was a companion for a few years, even though she was sickly and distant most of the time. Nature and animals had helped her survive without people. She wondered if Addition Jones had survived the same way.

"Thank you for listening and telling me about him. There's nothing I wouldn't do for you," Nell said impulsively to Margaret, grabbing her hands and squeezing them. Their hearts called out to each other from their unfulfilled places and they became best friends.

"Yes," Nell thought, "I will always be grateful to Addition Jones."

*

One morning, after the housework was done and they were wondering what to do with themselves, Margaret offered to drive Nell out to the old Smith farm.

She stopped the buggy on the knoll overlooking the farm and they stared down at the burned-out shell of a house and the silent, neglected buildings below. In a few minutes, Nell's eyes moved past the tragedy. She noticed the fields around the barns were wild and untamed, full of tall grass, dense with young trees. She looked at the wildflowers blooming around the old fence posts. Somehow, this place called out to her in a lovely, strange, wild way. She felt an answering joy rise up in her.

She glanced over at Margaret to see what she was feeling. Margaret looked somber, as befitted the occasion. She looked as though she was witnessing a funeral. Nell hastily pulled the beginnings of a smile off her face and stared somberly ahead, too.

After a while, Margaret clucked to the horse. She guided the buggy slowly and sedately down into the overgrown yard as though they were a funeral hearse carrying a casket.

Flower scented silence surrounded them. Sunlight dappled the ruins of the charred house, the faded red barn and weathered sheds. As if in a dream, Nell stepped down from the buggy. She heard Margaret's voice chiding her from a distance, but she ignored it, choosing instead to follow the feeling of strange joy rising slowly and steadily within her as she circled the black ruins of the house.

Her practical mind quickly took stock of the useable lumber left in the shell of the house. Then she turned towards the barn and sheds. She wandered everywhere, examining everything while the pull of the place held her in its grip. A revolutionary idea was forming in her mind. She quickened her pace, looking everything over and over again until Margaret was worn out with following her. At last, she turned to Margaret and smiled. Margaret stepped back a pace.

Color stained Nell's pale cheeks. Her large gray eyes glistened with eagerness. Margaret returned the smile, pleased with the change bringing such vitality to her new friend, but puzzled as to the cause.

Her smile slowly faded. A cautious frown replaced it. Something was wrong. She shouldn't have brought Nell out here. It was a bad idea. How could anybody feel good on this cursed farm? She watched in horror as Nell threw her arms out wide and turned a slow circle in the weed-filled yard.

"Redemption! I'm going to redeem this farm. No more curses, no more hate, no more pain, just flowers blooming and birds singing!" She shouted the promise into the air, her voice filled with exultation.

Margaret recoiled in shock. Nell wanted this place, this hell farm? She shook her head no, but Nell ignored her. Margaret found her voice and shouted, "No, no, no, no, no! You can't make anything up to Addition Jones. He's gone! Your father was the culprit! You don't have to pay for your father's sins! Jones is probably dead somewhere by now and he will never know about anything you do anyway!"

She pointed out the obvious problems to Nell.

"You can never buy the land, and to improve it for him won't make up for what was done to him! You need security now that you're alone! What if he was to come back?"

Nell didn't argue with her. She was listening to her heart. It was singing a strange new song. It told her that this was her new home, her new beginning, the one she had yearned for all of her life, and all would be well.

Suddenly, a breeze came up. Nell heard the quick flowing sound of laughing children rushing past her in it. But that wasn't possible, was it? She shrugged. Maybe it was angels, validating the sureness of her instincts. She laughed with them, turning in another slow circle, flinging her arms out wide.

Redemption would be a good thing for this old, bad farm. And for her. And for him. All three of them would benefit in different ways! Maybe she would call it Redemption Farm. At last she was filled with new purpose.

She realized she would always need something or someone to take care of. Someone to plan a future for. It was ingrained in her basic nature, like the need to breathe. She accepted it in her soul, and knew in that instant that her nature had been bent and formed for this farm and this time. This was her destiny and her place.

Anyway, what else did she have to hold on to? A bad bargain with a shadow man she would never meet was better than the loneliness she'd endure if she went back to the old farm.

Margaret saw the look on her face and gave up trying to talk her out of it. This place had cast some kind of strange spell over her new friend. She just wanted to get Nell away from this cursed farm so she could come back to her senses.

For the next few days, Margaret and Claude tried to talk Nell out of the idea of bringing life back to the old, abandoned Smith farm.

"Nothing good has ever happened out there," they said.

"Everybody knows that place is cursed!" they said.

"How are you going to do it? Do you realize how much money and work it will take?"

Gray steel shining in her eyes, she looked at them with dogged determination mixed with desperation. She had never argued with anyone before.

She explained, "I'll sell the home farm. That should give me enough money to get started, and I'll go as far as I can with it. I have other money, too. "

Nothing they said could persuade her to give up the idea. One day Nell grabbed Margaret's arm, her gray eyes wide with tears.

"You don't know how lonely I've been! All my life there's been no one except my mother, and she was too sick to love me or anything else very much. Then she died. Until Addition Jones' name was spoken into my life, there was nothing except land, vegetables, and animals to love me. I have to build a house out there. There's something absolutely right about it. I am doing the right thing and somehow, I know doing this will change things for the good of others someday. I can't go back to the farm I grew up on and stay there! I would die of loneliness."

Margaret knew the words were wrenched from deep within Nell's soul.

She set her mouth in a grim line and nodded. The next morning, Nell left for her old home. There was a lot to do before she could leave the old farm behind forever and start over in Cross Grove.

*

She drove the buggy into the silent, empty yard and stopped. She'd sold the cows and chickens before she set out to find Addition Jones. Neighbors took the cats. She kept the horse and buggy, though their best years were behind them.

The tired little farm was just the same, but she was changed, and there was a lot of work to do. There was a time and a purpose for everything, now that she was starting over.

She offloaded her supplies on the front doorstep, drove to the barn, unhitched the buggy and led the horse to the pasture. She filled the water trough for the horse. When the trough was full, she stared down into the water at her reflection, just as she'd done since she was tall enough to look into it. It was still her mirror.

Musing, she remembered watching the girl she once was changing in the water mirror through the years. The images came one after another, solemn and sure. Suddenly an image of herself with smears of blue paint on her face and in her hair floated to the surface of the water. Startled, she gasped and stared at the image intently. It was her all right. But different. The paint on her face and in her hair made her look wild and free-and beautiful!

She caught an impression of heat and fear of the unknown and something akin to love. Its flash burned her. Startled, she jumped back from the water trough. When she looked in the water again, the image was gone.

She looked around. She told herself she was imagining things. Just like she used to, back when she was a child staring into the water. She had imagined children playing and laughing back then, too. Well, maybe her imaginary playmates were disguised angels. Who knew?

She turned towards the house with new purpose. There was work to be done. She went to the kitchen and put her food away. Then she went through the house and made a list in her mind of all she needed to accomplish.

She took down the curtains, washed and pegged them on the clothesline to dry. She shined windows. She swept and mopped after dragging all the furniture and bedding out to the barn. It was long, slow work. When the curtains were dry, she folded and stacked them on the kitchen counter.

For days she worked, emptying out the house and cleaning, until one morning, her mother's bedroom was all that was left. She padded on silent feet through the empty house until she stood in front of the door.

For the first time in years, she turned the knob and pushed the door open. Her mother's faint scent wafted through the stale air. She stood in the doorway, remembering. After the funeral, she'd dusted and remade the bed with clean sheets and laid out her mother's hairbrush and comb on the dresser. The curtains rustled that day, a spring breeze winding its carefree way through the open windows. She'd set a small vase of wildflowers on the nightstand by the empty bed. The breeze played with them, ruffling their petals.

She took that as sign that her mother was happy to be free of her eternal sickroom.

She worked until she banished the smells of lingering illness and hopeless despair, replacing them with fresh air and the light, flowery scent of her mother's cologne.

*

The sun was setting by the time she emptied out the bedroom. The fine, pink lace curtains and the frail, curved furniture were out in the barn, along with the rag rugs. The hairbrush and comb set were packed in the carpet bag Nell found in the back of her mother's closet. The carpet bag sat in the living room alongside the few other things she wanted to keep. It sat beside the pallet she'd made herself to sleep on. She wouldn't let the house be hers any longer. If she gave into one little thing, she might end up staying here forever

*

She inspected the house. It was empty except for her few belongings. Everything was clean and orderly. She was ready for flight. There was just one last thing to be done, a thing she both hoped for and dreaded. It was

63

something she'd wondered about for years. Now it was time to find out.

She went outside to pace the yard and gather her courage. She listened to the silence, testing it before she went to the barn, removed the claw foot hammer from her father's toolbox, and carried it back to the house. Sunshine lit the silent, empty rooms. They smelled of bleach and peace and sunshine. Empty and clean.

Her heart pounded as she walked down the hallway, hiding the hammer in a fold of her skirt, as though someone was watching her. She tiptoed to her father's bedroom door, turned the cheap brass knob, and opened it carefully. She'd emptied it and cleaned it out right after the parlor, the only other place he always made his own whenever he was in the house.

She slipped inside the room and shut the door behind her. The smell of his drunken rampages still permeated the air. She was in his room, she hoped for the last time, with a purpose in mind she knew would enrage him if he were alive.

The hot, stinking air in the room closed in on her. Sweat beaded her forehead. She inched across the empty room and opened the closet door. The empty closet was still filled with the stench of his clothes and boots, layered with alcohol and rage. She knelt on the closet floor and carefully applied the hammer to a nail in a board in a back corner. The nail gave way with a snarling whine of protest as she yanked it out. She jumped back, startled. It sounded like her father protesting what she was doing! She breathed in gasps until her courage and anger returned. Using the hammer as leverage, she jerked the board up and threw it across the room as hard as she could. She gave a grim little smile at the "thwack" the board made hitting the plaster wall; she didn't need to turn to see the deep dent the board gouged out when it hit.

She leaned over and peered down in the small, dark hole. It was still there! The old bastard didn't get to do away with it before she could get to it. She let out a noisy sigh of relief and instantly clapped a hand over her mouth until quiet reigned again.

She reached in, lifted the old cigar box out of its hiding place, and brought it up into the light of day. No more hiding a damn thing! He was standing before his maker and unable to hide so much as a wart now.

She stared at the yellow, aged label and the palm trees on the cigar box. Silent, bitter laughter rushed through her. He thought she never knew about the cigar box under the board in his closet. All those years after her mother died, and he still wouldn't tell her about it, even when he was dying! She wondered what other secrets he'd carried to his grave.

Well, at least two of them were out in the open now. Addition Jones and the secret in the box she held. And both of them just might make life a whole lot better for her! One already was. At least there was hope now with him gone!

She set the cigar box down, retrieved the board and nailed it back in place. Emptiness was the only thing beneath the board now. It was just a hollow, hidden place with no secrets or selfishness hiding in it anymore.

When she finished, she stood and shut the closet door. The final sound of it closing was pleasing. She looked around his room, picked up the cigar box and walked out, closing his bedroom door behind her.

She carried the cigar box and hammer down the hall and into the empty kitchen. She set the cigar box down on the countertop, grabbed a dish towel and wiped the thick dust off of it. She took a deep breath before she opened the lid and looked inside.

In stunned amazement, she lifted the thick wad of money out of the box, turning it around in her hands, marveling at the size of it. She carefully removed the paper bands from around the money and smoothed the bills out into rows by denomination on the kitchen counter.

There was a lot of money! Had he robbed a bank? Probably. Anger rushed through her as she stared down at the green bills. Every one of them represented something her father made her mother and her do without. She'd gone without tools and so many other things that would have made life on this farm so much easier.

She could go on for hours, listing the losses she and her mother took because of Grady Millers vanity and selfishness, but she ordered her thoughts to stop. There was plenty of time for that later. She wasn't going to waste one more second of time on him right now, because she had just stolen back from him what belonged to her and her mother, and it was going to go to a damn good cause—her freedom from him!

She remembered her mother's love of the Bible and the words she lived by. Forgive and forget. Well, she had a few words of her own for the old bastard, now that his lifeline of pity, attached to her through her mother's weak, puling words, was gone.

Nell shouted into the empty house, "Vengeance is mine, saith the Lord!"

"Vengeance is mine, saith' the Lord!" she shouted again, her voice cracking with the pain of independence, of a child letting go of a mother and father, for all children harbor a little bit of love, if only a bare scrap, for their mother and father. The genetics of inheritance cannot and will not be denied, even under the evilest of circumstances. Life must go on. And it took love to help the good conquer the bad. Her words echoed through the empty house, taking on meaning and heat, then dissolving in the thin, clean air.

This money belonged to her, legally. There were no relatives left on either side. There were no other heirs. She was it. She looked inside the cigar box again. It stunk, just like the cigars he smoked and the cigarettes he rolled one after the other, drinking his cheap whiskey, swaggering around the house bragging on "his property," and himself.

In the bottom of the cigar box was a small, yellowed slip of paper. She picked it up and unfolded it. She studied the name and address written on it in his elegant handwriting.

After turning it this way and that, she shrugged and laid the thin, worn piece of paper carefully beside the money. It was no one she knew. Not yet, anyway. But if he'd kept it and worn the paper thin, then surely it was the name of somebody important to him, no doubt somebody he'd wronged.

She sorted the money out, folded it neatly, and placed it and the worn piece of paper in her purse. Then she carried the cigar box outside, tossed it on the ground, lit a match and threw it in the empty box. The old, dry cigar box burst into flames, as though it couldn't leave fast enough. She watched it burn, poking it with the scuffed toe of her shoe to keep the flames going until the box lay in black ashes at her feet. She stomped the warm ashes into the ground until they mixed with dust and dirt and disappeared. "From dust to dust," she thought grimly. She went back in the house, picked up her purse and headed to the barn to hitch up the buggy. It was time to take a trip to town.

*

The only bank in the small town of Prairie Creek was in a small wood structure on the corner of Main and 1st Street. The thin, bare windows on each side of the door glared in the sunlight. She stopped the buggy at the hitching rail and got out. A few people walking by stared at her, but she didn't pay any attention to them.

The bell above the door jingled when she stepped inside the bank. Nell closed the door behind her and looked around. The only teller in sight finally looked up from the newspaper he was reading, straightened his tie, and stepped up to the teller's window.

"May I help you?" he asked, looking down his nose at her through his glasses.

"Yes sir. I want to open a bank account," she stated briskly.

"Well, we don't usually allow women to open accounts in their own name. Is your husband with you?" he drawled in a bored voice.

"I don't have a husband. Never married. My name is Nell Miller, and I intend to open a bank account today. If not here, then someplace else."

She pulled the huge wad of money out of her purse and slapped it down on the counter. The teller's eyes widened.

"Just a minute."

He hurried to the back of the bank and stepped into an office, closing the door behind him. A minute passed before the office door opened again, and a short, rotund man followed the teller out. He was smiling.

"I'm Tom Preston, president of this here bank. You said you are Miss Nell Miller?"

She nodded nervously. This was her first time in a bank.

"Would you mind stepping into my office so we can discuss a matter of the greatest importance? That is, after Joe gets through opening your personal account for you? I've been meaning to contact you. Went out to your place after your father died, but there wasn't anybody around." He peered at her wisely. "Perhaps you were away visiting relatives?"

She managed to nod and stay calm while the teller opened her account. His attitude had changed rapidly to one of helpfulness instead of disdain.

When they were finished, he handed over her new account book and escorted her into Preston's office. She found herself perched on the edge of a large, overstuffed, brown leather chair across from the bank president himself.

Mr. Preston said, "I apologize for not having a more suitable chair for you in here, but it's mostly men I talk with." He rattled the stack of papers in front of him importantly, cleared his throat and began.

"Miss Miller, you know your grandfather left his farm and everything he owned to you, don't you? I've been wondering why we haven't seen you in here before to pick up the paperwork and the deeds to the properties. We held the notes on both farms until they were paid off. Your grandfather left both deeds here in a safety deposit box. And there's some money, too. You are the sole heir to all of it."

Nell stared at him while her mind worked it out. Her mother was an only child. She was their only grandchild. There was a substantial amount of money in the beginning, but she thought her father used it all up over the years.

Evidently, her grandfather knew the kind of man her father was and protected what he owned from him...for her... Tears threatened to spill. Now that the crying was back, she never knew when it was going to start. Hastily she grabbed a handkerchief from her purse, wiped her eyes and blew her nose. The banker waited patiently until she was done.

"The farms are still intact, even though your father tried to sell them. But the deeds were in your name, and he needed your signature on them..."

After the papers were signed and all was in order, Nell thanked Mr. Preston and placed the deeds and other legal papers in her grandfather's safety deposit box.

"Of course, it is your safety deposit box now," the banker gestured grandly. She stepped back out into the bank and asked the teller to add the money she inherited to her new bank account.

She left the bank with a light heart, a quick step, a fat bank account, and her head held high. She was a rich woman now, a woman of property! She wanted to dance a jig in the street. She thought about the farm. Now that she had money to do what really needed to be done, she could finish it and leave it the way she wanted it to be. It needed deeper work to rid it of the penury she and her mother endured because of her father's evil ways.

Joy flooded her. She was going to start over with all new...everything. All new! No ugly reminders of the dismal, hopeless past. She would clean up her little farm, using her father's cigar box money; why, she'd be using his money to eradicate his evil! Her mother might snivel, but her grandparents would approve! Maybe she would name it Hopeful Farm when it was done.

She stopped at the general store to buy salt and a few basic things. She set them on the counter. Suddenly they looked scanty. Not enough. She hesitated. Now she could afford the softness of what she imagined good fabric to be. And towels and some sort of fragrance.... She added two bars of handmade soap, a huge, thick white towel, and a pair of house slippers to her necessities.

Still, they didn't seem to be enough. She was owed, and she was paid. Better late than never. She intended to enjoy being paid after a lifetime of working for nothing. Quickly she added a box of rich chocolate drops, two hair combs, a hairbrush, and two soft white cotton nightgowns.

She handed over the money and inquired, "Is there a respectable young man or boy I can hire to help me out at my farm? I need things moved and general help."

She hired a boy from town to come out to the farm the next day and haul away the things stored in the barn. The boy arrived early the next morning, eager to carry away them away. He readily agreed to come back and run errands and work around the farm.

Nell began the deeper level of work she intended to do. Money was no object now. Maybe she would sell the farm, maybe not. She wouldn't decide anything until it was cleaned up and done up the way she always wanted it to be. The most important thing was to cleanse the farm free it of its old, hopeless misery.

She was responsible for turning the place into a hopeful farm, full of promise for whoever lived there next, and she would use Grady Miller's money to do it! She laughed behind her hand at the thought. Her father's evil was a curse still permeating the farm. Now his money was going to change that curse back into the goodness everything on the farm deserved. He was providing the means to do whatever it took to stop his evil intentions from reaching beyond the grave to poison and torture anyone living here ever again!

She washed wood, scrubbed and polished floors until they shined. She sent the errand boy to town for paint and other things. She set him to painting the inside of the house while she hoed and raked and cleaned and watered outside.

The sunny days flew by in a flurry of work until one day, she stood in the front yard with a "Hopeful Farm" - For Sale" sign in her hand.

She looked around. There was no trace left of her father or mother or her on the property. The house smelled of flowers and new paint and cleanliness. Gone was the feeling of travail, rage and misery that was once embedded in the very walls. The picket fence was repaired and freshly painted. White painted rocks lined the path to the porch. The barn and the shed were cleared out, cleaned out, repaired and painted. The garden was weeded behind a sturdy new fence. Vegetables grew in neat rows.

She sent the boy for livestock and feed. There was new chicken wire around the chicken coop and run. Young chickens pecked happily at their feed in the run. The fences around the fields were still in good shape. She remembered her grandfather fencing them when she was a small girl. The fencing was still solid.

She didn't do anything to her grandparent's property. She could afford to keep it now, and she wanted it kept just the way it was when she was young. She went in their empty house and felt the strength of the love they once provided her. She was almost too young to remember when they died of the fever. She couldn't bear for someone else to live there, for they would inevitably make changes. She hired a handyman to come out and take care of the property. He was to repair the barns and the house, get everything back in good shape, and maintain it exactly as it was. He was to care take it and make sure nobody bothered anything. She arranged his monthly payments through the bank.

She hammered the stake with the hand painted for sale sign nailed on it into the ground. Then she sent the errand boy into town to pass the word around. Within a month, she sold the farm to a busy little hen of a woman and her lanky, somber husband. They rode into the yard in a small, battered wagon that had seen better days.

Their sharp, hungry eyes roamed the fields and garden and the milk cow over and over. They counted the chickens and measured the two pigs. They rubbed their fingers restlessly together, and his Adam's apple bobbed madly while they bargained with her on the price of the little farm. She could tell they wanted to get their hands on the place and make it their own as fast as they could because the vegetables were ready, and the fruit trees dead ripe.

Before long it would be fall, and they would have good work ahead of them. Nell gave them a bargain price on the farm. After the papers were signed, the couple left. They would return in three days to take over the farm. Nell spent those days roaming the farm, remembering herself as a child during her different ages. She wandered past the tall cottonwood tree shading the corner of the yard. All that was left of the board swing was a frayed piece of rope. She smoothed the frayed rope with her hand.

Her mother insisted her father put the swing up for Nell when he was in one of his rare good moods. Of course he made it to fit him. But no matter. She remembered swinging in it, high to the sky, making up songs. Her father liked to sing, too. Her hair felt good when it flew out behind her. She remembered watching her bare, brown toes sticking out in front of her. She ran her bare feet through the smooth, silky dirt packed around the tree roots, remembering making little pens out of sticks, putting baby chicks inside the pens. The chicks always got out.

And Sam. Sam's fur was red and soft. He was an old stray dog that showed up at their place, hungry and tired. She kept him through his last few years, even though her father flew mad every time he saw him. She hid Sam from her father more than once. She sighed. There wasn't much more to remember than that. Just the never-ending work, the terrible loneliness of having no companions, and the careful, tender drudgery of taking care of her sick, whining mother.

She never wanted to come back here again. Her life was starting over in a new place. When the couple who bought the farm arrived, she

wished them well, climbed into her buggy and
drove away without a backward glance.

Chapter 5. A Town Without Pity

Factories
Formulas

While Nell was finishing up her old life, Claude and Margaret were paving the way for her new life in Cross Grove.

"Nell is going to build a house out on Addition Jones' old place."

Claude calmly announced the news to the old men sitting around the checkerboard in the back of the store. Like the Pharisees of old, the store emptied out like magic. The old men scattered and thundered around the town, spreading the news.

Storms of dissent followed, and Cross Grove quickly became divided into for and against camps. Claude and Margaret monitored the angry talk.

"She's a fool! So what if her father did Addition Jones wrong? Her story might not be true! And if it is, why should she try to make up for what her father did?"

Claude and Margaret nodded humbly and didn't answer. They just listened. They knew people were mad about a piece of the town's history being proven wrong by Nell's story, and if she moved out to the farm, it would rub the wrong they'd ignored and the man they'd hated so readily in their faces.

The town stayed firmly divided. One faction was dead set against Nell building a house on Addition Jones' farm. The other faction was willing to accept it, but did not approve of the idea.

"It isn't our business to tell other people how to live their lives," they stated righteously to anyone willing to listen.

"Hate is a hard thing to dissolve, for ignorance is easily astounded and offended and way too quick to defend itself," Claude remarked dryly to Margaret when they were alone at home.

"People have the silliest need to be right no matter the cost!" Margaret agreed. "No redemption wanted!"

Underneath their words, the town's real problem was the moral dilemma surrounding Addition Jones. Cross Grove had ignored his existence as a human being for years. Then they rebuffed him by insisting he was a murderer.

They liked thinking of themselves as godly, upright citizens who always made correct judgments. But exhaustion has its own form of limited perseverance, and Claude and Margaret hoped it would wear them out over time. Each night they looked at each other across the dinner table and sighed. It was going to be a long road, but it had to be enough to begin with.

*

The bedroom was ready and waiting. Margaret helped Nell carry her things up. Nell returned in a new black buggy pulled by a sedate, fairly young horse. The old horse was let out to pasture on the farm she sold. She paid the new owners for his upkeep and told them she'd be back to check on him. Claude was pleased Nell planned to stay with them while her new house was being built out on the farm.

It didn't take long for him to figure out that Margaret and Nell were very much alike, and he liked his wife having the companionship of another woman who understood her. Besides, between the two of them, his clothes were kept spanking clean and perfect, and he was enjoying the best dinners and desserts of his life.

Nell and Margaret drove out to the farm almost every day. They went over every inch of the place and made their plans. Some of the lumber from the burned out shell of the house was still good, but Nell decided not to use it because of the curse it bore. She'd just got through cleaning up one farm with a curse on it!

They salvaged a few pictures and kitchen utensils from the burned-out shell and stored them carefully in the little back room in the faded barn. Nell knew the little room was Addition Jones' real home the minute she stepped into it.

Claude planned to take over when they were ready. He would see to the hiring of the men needed to build the simple, one-story house Nell settled on. Word of the hiring went around Cross Grove, and people agreed all over again that Nell was crazy.

The old men in the general store were jubilant. They finally had a new subject to gossip about instead of crops, animals, and weather. Claude kept his mouth shut and grinned at them. Sometimes he shrugged his shoulders and sighed.

"What can you do with women when they've made up their minds to something?"

The rest of the men shook their heads in sympathy and sighed along with him.

Before long, the thrifty, practical farm women around Cross Grove started driving out to the farm to look things over. Their husbands could use the extra work after the harvest was in.

The men hired on and went to work, and their women rolled up their sleeves and gave Margaret and Nell a hand with the things they needed. Time flew by as the work expanded to include a new shed and a smokehouse.

*

Fall set in. A day finally came when Nell, Margaret, and Claude stood together in the sunlit yard admiring the changes in the farm. There was no sign a tragedy had ever touched the place. The well was clean and deep. The barn and outbuildings repaired or replaced.

The remnants of the old house had been carefully burned down to ashes and scattered across the fields. Then the ground where the burned-out house once stood was cleaned, smoothed and leveled. New dirt and grass seed was added. New grass was already growing. Nell's cheerful butter yellow house stood dead center on the spot where the burned out house once stood. Flowers and such would wait until spring. Winter was coming soon.

There were long windows in the front of the house, framed with white shutters. The windows let the morning and noon day sun in. A wraparound porch with a deep roof, wide, white, welcoming steps, and snow-white railing embraced the little house, providing summer shade and protection from winter weather. The roof was peaked to ward off snow. The back entry was inside a small mudroom with steps leading up to the back door of the house. A root cellar was beside the mudroom, close and convenient. Winter wood had been chopped into sixteen-inch bush cords and neatly stacked under a shed roof a few feet from the house. The flat, wide roof boards were pulled down in the spring, and easily put back up in the winter. Large firewood holders were built into each side of the fireplace so Nell could stock up and not have to go out often for wood when the temperature dropped.

The townspeople scoured the farm, the fields and buildings, but whenever Nell found something of Addition Jones, she carried it to the barn and locked it in his little room. Some of the workers and their wives were curious and asked about his room, but she was adamant that no one go in there. Somehow, she knew she shouldn't show the people who had wronged him any more of him than was necessary.

The old stories about Addition Jones had flared up and spread through Cross Grove at the beginning of the renovation. But the truth Nell told stood in the way of the stories, and they reluctantly settled into whispers.

*

The whole town was invited to Nell's housewarming. Some would come, others wouldn't. It was the way of life. She was confident most of them would show up because they were practical people who knew where their bread was buttered.

Nell had changed. The blinders she'd worn during her life of isolation were gone.

People asked her about her life before Cross Grove, and how she happened to be a woman with so much money. She told them nothing; only she, Claude and Margaret knew anything about her history. After a while, they quit asking.

She knew they quit because there was money to be made, and she had it, wherever it came from; it was smart and profitable to stay on her good side and mind their own business. Knowing this didn't make Nell bitter. It merely eased her way, and she was glad of it.

Soon the rooms of the house and the yard would fill with people. The big table in the kitchen was stacked with pies and cakes and pitchers of lemonade. The ice box was filled to the brim with meat ready to barbeque over the fire pits the men set up near the corral.

Bowls of potato salad rested in chunks of ice in washtubs in the pantry. Large pans of baked beans steamed on the big white iron stove. Everyone was bringing their own silverware, plates, and glasses, plus a little something extra to add to the celebration.

Mrs. Donelson was bringing jars of her special crisp, sweet pickles. Jake Watson had volunteered to baste the meat with his secret barbeque sauce. Vincent Green and his sons were bringing tables and chairs from the Methodist church and setting them up.

Nell looked at her new house and sighed contentedly. She was starting over. She'd made the right decision. She knew she was soft-hearted in many ways. She believed in Heaven, where her mother dwelt. She could do this. She was strong and healthy. She was used to living by herself and taking care of a farm. She knew well how to mend fences, grow a garden, and take care of livestock. Her father taught her how to use a gun, her mother how to sing hymns when she was happy. Yes, she could do this.

This place called out to her. Somebody's future lay here. Her instincts assured her she was readying this place for others who needed her help. They would come here after she was done on Earth. She knew it was true.

She was a late bloomer who'd let her heart turn to the only choice she could find, for better or worse. Today, it looked like it was for better. This time, she would have friends while she lived on a farm. Margaret was her best friend. And most people in Cross Grove decided to be friendly to her. She didn't give a damn what the reason was.

She thought about Addition Jones. This was his place, always would be, whether he was dead or alive. When she discovered his little room in the back of the barn, she knew to leave it exactly like it was. Feeling like an intruder, she crept into his room and looked around. She'd heard the stories and knew the small space she was standing in was the only home he'd ever known.

Sorrow welled up in her for the lonely years he'd endured because of her father. She knew about that kind of isolation and deadly loneliness. She'd slipped back out and closed the door behind her. Before the house construction began, she padlocked his door and kept the key so no one could open it and snoop through his belongings.

"Are you happy, Nell?" Margaret interrupted her thoughts. Nell smiled, grabbed Margaret's hands, and danced her in a circle.

*

Late that evening, Nell stood on her new porch watching the sun set behind the newly painted barn. This would be her first night alone on his farm. Her ears still rang with the laughter the farm was filled with earlier in the day.

The men proudly showed off their skilled carpentry to their wives while their children ran and played. The old men sat together at one table, chewing slowly and ruminating while watching everyone.

The women admired the shiny, honey-colored hardwood floors in the large living room and the sheer white curtains over the wide kitchen windows. They admired the fluffy featherbeds covering the double beds in the two bedrooms. Nell's mother's elegant handmade quilts were layered across the beds and some of the women asked to copy the patterns her mother used to make them.

Nell shivered in the night air. It wouldn't be long before fall was gone. Winter was coming. She sniffed the air. It blew sweet with the promise of first snow. She slipped through the front door and closed it behind her.

*

Nell sat at the kitchen table sipping hot coffee, watching the snow falling outside the window. The snow fell like cornmeal, sifting over the ground and trees and roofs of the sheds and barn. She remembered the old saying, "Snow like meal, snow a great deal."

There were chickens in the coop and a milk cow named Susie. Cords of wood were curing, stacked in neat rows in back of the house. Hay and grain for the horse and cow were stored in the barn.

When the fall weather had turned cold, Claude and a bunch of townspeople had come out to the farm and butchered a hog for her.

After they bled it, they cut it open and removed its insides. Then the men dipped the hog in scalding water over and over again and scraped the hair from the hog's hide. Then they singed the hog over the fire to get the last of the fine hair off of the skin, laid it out on a large table, and cut the meat into large pieces.

The women carried the meat into the bright, new kitchen and laid it out on tables. First, they trimmed the fat off. The fat was white as snow. The hog had been healthy. The pieces of fat were added to the large black kettle setting on a grill over a fire pit outside. The fat was boiled down until it liquefied. When the hot fat cooled down enough, it would be cut it into squares, wrapped in butcher paper and cloth and stored in the root cellar.

The pig skin was made into cracklings. It was cut up into bite size pieces, then dropped into the pot of hot lard. The pieces puffed up and browned instantly. Scooped out with a metal slotted spoon, laid out and salted, they made a fine snack for everybody.

The women cut the meat into smaller and smaller pieces. They seasoned the hams and bacon and pork roasts and packed them into bags. The men carried the bags of meat out to the new smokehouse and hung them up for curing. The pork chops and other cuts of meat were layered into the short spindle wood barrels waiting on the cool, dark floor of the pantry. Each layer of meat was packed into a barrel and salt brine poured over it. The meat was stirred so the brine would touch all parts of it.

When the meat barrel was full, a layer of four to six inches of melted lard was poured over the top of it. The lard cooled and hardened, sealing the meat in the brine so the air couldn't get to it. Last, a clean white square of cotton cloth was placed over the barrel and tied. The cloth would keep insects and other curious little creatures from getting into the barrel and ruining the meat and lard in it.

They made sausage out of the leftovers, using sage and spice measures from Nell's grandmother's recipe. People shared their harvest bounty with Nell. Shiny jars of pickles and jams stood in orderly rows on the new pantry shelves. Crates of individually wrapped potatoes, wrapped so they couldn't touch each other and rot, were stacked in the pantry.

Strings of dried beans and crabapples hung in neat rows from the pantry ceiling. A row of small crocks in the back held fermenting sauerkraut and sulfured apples.

Margaret and Claude wanted Nell to spend the winter with them because the farm was a few miles out of town. Sometimes the roads filled with heavy snow, making it impossible to leave the farm for long stretches of time. Nell was prepared. She'd spent most of her life alone out on a farm. She already knew how to survive worse things than a temporarily closed road.

*

A few days passed. Nell was getting used to her new routine. Everything was done, nothing was needed, and the chores took just a small amount of her time each day. She found herself wandering through the house, looking for work. Maybe she could find something to sew. Before long, her sewing machine was set up in the spare bedroom. She made a couple of trips to town to buy materials and the other things she needed to make a dress. She oiled her mother's treadle sewing machine, put the bobbin in, and set to work.

A few days later, Nell held up the finished dress. The simple, plain, serviceable winter dress she planned had somehow turned into a fancy blue wool dress made for church, courting, or going visiting. She examined the full waist, the ankle length hem, the full sleeves and black velvet collar and cuffs. She'd pulled the skirt into a bustle in the back, causing the waistline to dip in the front. It was a design to flatter the back and posterior. She glanced out the window. It was time to go see Margaret and explain her idea.

*

"It's lovely. Well done, Nell!"

Margaret turned the dress this way and that, running her fingers over the flawless seams while Nell explained.

"I've seen the plain housedresses a lot of the women wear. I know they need serviceable farm dresses, but they also need something nicer, something better to wear for special occasions. Something dreams are made of. And, I think that some of them don't like to sew, or aren't too good at it, and others are too tired to fuss with a new look.

Since we both like to sew, and are good at it, maybe we could make a few dresses in the winter when we're not busy and display them in the front window of the general store. What do you think?"

Margaret caught Nell's enthusiasm.

"What a good idea!" She paced back and forth while Nell waited.

"Hmmm... It might or might not work, but we could give it a try! What price do we put on them?" they asked each other at the same time.

In a matter of a few hours, they converted one of Margaret's upstairs bedrooms into a sewing room. That way, they could work alone or together at either house. By the first week of December, there were four winter dresses on display in the front window of the general store. The deceptively simple dresses were made of high-quality wools and velvets in shades of pearl gray, dark rose, forest green and nautical blue.

Each dress was a classic design, with ankle length flared skirts, long sleeves, fitted bodices, and a variety of necklines. Nell's blue wool with its bustle, full sleeves buttoning at the wrist, and a demure sweetheart neckline was first. Their second dress was gray wool with a gored skirt, a round neckline inset with pink lace, with the lace repeated at the edge of the cuffs, and white bone buttons at the wrist.

Their third dress was a forest green challis with dainty white lace tatting framing the square neckline and black velvet cuffs buttoned with tiny pearls. The fourth dress was dark rose velvet with striped beige and black silk cuffs and a beige silk scalloped collar at the jewel neckline.

Claude applauded their work. The prices he insisted they put on the dresses made them almost swoon.

"You have to be well paid for your skills, hard work and imagination." he insisted. "You're designers, you know. I don't know how much fashion designers earn in Chicago, but you're going to be well paid in corn country!"

The old men stared at the four dresses in the window and muttered darkly to each other.

"Our women will start thinking about too many fancy things, and they'll turn lazy and won't even get supper on the table! Why, they'll start thinking about goin' to Paris on one of them ships and forget to wash our clothes!"

The quiet farm men in their work clothes came in the store as usual. With stoic, weather-beaten farmer's faces that never gave away what they were thinking, they studied the Christmas dresses. Then they went home and told their wives about them. In a few days, the window was bare. Margaret and Nell were excited by their success. They planned to make more dresses in the spring.

Nell spent Christmas day with Claude and Margaret. They exchanged new dress ideas nonstop while they basted the large, wild turkey roasting in the oven. Claude took their minds off their dress business by carving raw potatoes into funny shapes to entertain them.

New Year's Day found Nell looking through the windows of her new house, watching sleet fall. The tapping sound of it was a thing she never grew tired of. She remembered the music the weather made in her childhood. She never felt alone when she heard sleet. Maybe it carried voices in it like she imagined back then. Nature had always been her faithful companion.

She fell asleep, covered with her mother's quilts, surrounded by the newness of the little yellow house, listening to the sounds in the sleet.

The coldest part of winter set in. Heavy winds blew. The land contracted, making cracking, popping noises. Nell kept the kerosene lamps lit. The flames in the fireplace danced with warmth. She took care of the animals and read and sewed while the winter winds howled around the cheerful, little yellow house, searching for entry and not finding it.

Other living beings counted on her for food and shelter, and she would not let them down. Each morning she heated water for the animals and poured it over the frozen water in their drinking pans and stock tanks.

When she crunched across the porch, down the wide steps and through the deep snow to the barn and sheds, the sound of her boots confirmed her existence. She was making a good way on the Earth, and God and anyone else who cared to listen could hear it.

It was a new, good feeling, a peaceful, clear time. Her father was paying the dues owed to redemption. She felt the shadows thinning in the cold winter sun glowing over the old farm as she worked and lived.

She felt the sun and Nature steadily working alongside her, thinning the shadows the Smiths, Cross Grove and her father had forced her and Addition Jones to live under. No more. This farm was becoming sacred to her.

Nature was more powerful than any evil. Sometimes she laughed in bittersweet elation.

March came and went, but winter never loosed its icy grip on the land. The old timers said it was a hard winter, the worst in years. They spent long hours in the general store comparing blizzards of the past to the storms this winter.

At last, the end of April brought a lessening of the snow and wind.

Chapter 6. The Secret Visitor

Candles
Consequences

Nell learned early in life never to waste anything. She kept a partially filled grain barrel and added hot water to it to make mash for the pigs and chickens. The scraps from the kitchen, except for the meat and bones, went into the barrel.

The grain mixture fermented over time into a rich swill. She dipped out a bucketful every few days and carried it to the pigs and chickens. They loved the treat and came running for it.

One day she dipped up a bucket of fermented swill and crunched through the snow to the pig pen. She watched them eat for a few minutes before she turned to go back to the house. As she turned, out of the corner of her eye, she saw something move.

All of a sudden, she had the strongest impression that whatever it was, wanted, needed to scare her. A chill ran across the back of her neck. She turned her eyes up to the knoll above the house and dropped the swill bucket in surprise.

A big man, dressed in black, sat motionless on his black horse under the oak tree. He was rangy, thin, all kinds of angles, as though he was starving, his big body a dark shadow on the big horse. He was watching her.

Her mind flashed to an image of her father sitting on a knoll above the place of the woman he wronged so greatly, and of the misery he caused her son. Wind gusted once through her mind. Then she knew, deep in her being. The child her father wronged still owned this farm.

She wanted to run to the house but forced herself to walk. She stepped up on the porch and casually picked up the loaded rifle she kept handy by the front door. She was familiar with guns, for her father taught her early to protect herself and her mother, his property, when he was gone. A woman living by herself never knew what she would have to deal with. Usually, it was only varmints or such, and to err on the side of caution was smart. She carried the gun boldly around the back of the house. She wanted to get a better look at the man. But he was gone.

The next morning, she hitched up the buggy and drove to Margaret's. Margaret cooked for them. They both liked to eat, and neither one ever gained an ounce from it. After they ate, Margaret poured fresh, hot coffee into their cups. A basket of warm apple fritters to snack on sat beside the colorful ceramic rooster dominating the middle of Margaret's kitchen table.

They strolled down the hall to the sewing room to examine their newly finished spring dresses. When they finished their inspection, Nell closed the sewing room door and leaned back against it.

"I have something to tell you."

Margaret glanced up from the dresses.

"I think I might have seen Addition Jones yesterday."

"What? No, it couldn't have been him!"

Margaret jumped up, her eyes wide.

"Why didn't you tell me when you first got here?"

Nell shrugged. "I don't know."

"No," said Margaret decisively, shaking her head.

"It couldn't have been him. He hasn't been seen in these parts for years. What happened?"

Nell described the rider sitting on the knoll above the house and how he watched her. Margaret ruminated.

"Maybe it was Addition Jones."

Nell sighed. "I have a feeling it was."

She shivered.

Margaret said, "Maybe it wasn't him, that's a possibility, too." Nell nodded hopefully.

Margaret offered, "Do you want to stay here? We can ride out to the farm and do the chores every morning. I don't like to think of you out there alone in case whoever he is comes back."

"I plan to stay put, but I'm going to keep my gun handy."

Silence fell as thoughts of the future ran through both their minds. They assumed Addition Jones would never return. And if the man Nell saw was him, what next?

"Let's not tell anybody except Claude," Nell said.

"Maybe it was just someone passing through. I'm almost positive it was! We don't want any more useless talk stirred up again!"

She changed the subject so Margaret wouldn't guess how much seeing the rider had affected her.

She did the chores as soon as she got home. She didn't have to boil water for the stock tanks since it seldom froze now. After the chores were done, she went back to the house and paced the floor. She wandered restlessly through each room. She pulled the curtains back from the windows and looked out, trying to escape from what she was thinking.

What if the man was Addition Jones? Wouldn't she welcome him? Wasn't she making atonement for her father's evil by building this house? Wasn't that much owed to Addition Jones, whether she got to live in it or not?

She'd felt pretty self-righteous when she built this house, she admitted to herself. Her motives were proper and holy and all that. Building the house was like erecting a clean tombstone over an old, dried up grave...a good thing.

Sooner or later, somebody would have resurrected this old farm. She just happened to be the first to begin it. Of course, she was the one with the most reason to do it. A strong sureness came over her. Others would carry on the tradition of healing this farm and its people after she was gone. She'd done the right thing.

Maybe Addition Jones was back and would take it from her. Well, so be it. But no one would ever again have to look at the charred ruins of the bitter life Addition Jones suffered before he fled. He was owed that much and more.

She'd built and moved into this house and filled it with warmth and life and common sense. *Like a person waiting for a beloved to return,* she thought. She dropped the curtain and stepped back from the window.

Her father...she felt a dark righteousness, standing in this house. She let herself remember his words. He'd confessed his sins to her because he wanted her to know and admire what a monster he was before he died. His handsome face was grotesque with vicious cruelty as he insisted she was his seed; that she carry on his inheritance of hate and become a monster herself. He'd looked up into her face, his dark eyes alight with envy that she was alive and he was dying, watching with glee the revulsion and horror stealing over her very being. He was giving himself one last chance to kill somebody on his way out. But he didn't succeed. Her soul had survived his evil intentions because of Addition Jones.

She knew all about him now. Their stories were the same. He didn't have any idea where his troubles came from, but she knew. Because of her father, they'd both grew up without love and the simple companionship and affection of friends and family. Like her, he'd been put to work on a farm and not allowed to leave or do anything else. Isolated, uneducated, and friendless, she had become more passive, doing without the comforts and closeness of a husband and children, while he fought back and ran away at an early age.

Maybe he'd found what he needed out in the world. She hoped so. Regardless, he'd been her unknown companion all her life, and that knowledge had carried her to Cross Grove and out to redeeming this farm.

Chapter 7. The Letter

Manifestation
Iron Ore

"Spring is a hopeful time of year!" Nell exulted as she strode across the land. The man hadn't been back. Most of the plants, birds, bees and animals were familiar. But someone long ago planted herbs for the animals out along the fence rows. An amazing amount of catnip, clover, wildflowers, and seed plants grew wild just as they pleased.

She started a garden, filling it with seeds and starters of peas, potatoes, corn and tomatoes. She planted cucumbers and green beans against tall fencing, leaving them free to climb at their own will.

She kept herself busy from daylight to dark, just the way she'd always lived. She relished it, thrived on it. She worked the farm and went to church and helped Margaret with their dressmaking business. It was a new life and a good one.

One Sunday morning she dressed for church and left the house. On impulse, she stopped the buggy on the knoll above the farm to admire the scene below. The chickens scratched contentedly in their fenced run. The house beamed a cheerful butter yellow in the sun. Flowers bloomed around the house. The garden was green and expectant, the buildings sharp-edged in their new paint. She smiled to herself as she clucked to the horse and curved the buggy from the knoll back towards the road.

Suddenly she jerked the buggy to a stop. In front of her was the dark rider she'd seen on the knoll. The horse he sat was big, rangy and black. The man was tall and thin and dressed in black. His straight, thick black hair fell in a shock over his heavy brows. He glared at her; his face swarthy, his wide mouth thinned down into a frown. His coal black eyes held flinty sparks of anger.

She stared into the angry black eyes above the high, hollow cheekbones and hawk nose, searching for any sign of humanity. His eyes burned into hers with contempt. A century of time dragged by. The hum of bees working the flowers by the buggy path roared in her ears. The smell of their horses and the creaking of the leather harness on the buggy registered loudly in her mind. Every detail, every smell, every noise etched itself into her mind.

Abruptly he moved and broke the spell. He cantered past her like she didn't exist, like all the time in the world belonged to him. He rode leisurely down into the farmyard. She twisted around on the buggy seat, watching him circle the house, barn, and buildings. He rode easily, a natural rider. He took his time and looked everything over. When he was done with his survey, he rode up the hill past her as though she didn't exist.

*

Nell was late for church. Heart pounding, she slipped into a back pew. The hymn ended. The long-winded preacher began a sermon she thought would never end. Her hands trembled on her Bible. She stared up at the preacher, not seeing him, not hearing a word. Her mind was reeling. Addition Jones was back, and she didn't like him. He wasn't the man she imagined him to be. She'd taken for granted she would like him, that he would like her too.

At last the service ended. Nell rushed up to Margaret and grabbed her hands, intending to tell her everything. Then in a split second, the need to tell on Addition Jones, a ridiculous name for the surly man she'd encountered, fell away from her.

She stood there, cold, aching and needy, side by side with her dark, silent companion. She'd planned to tell Margaret the dark man was back, but she couldn't. The whole town hated him, always would. Her heart broke. She shuddered. She wouldn't tell on him again. He was hers, no matter what happened.

She shuddered again and pinched her lips shut. She couldn't give him up, and she wouldn't. He was part of her soul now. She would just have to wait and see what happened.

Margaret waited for her to say something. When Nell didn't speak, Margaret pulled her hands loose from Nell's grip and smiled at her. She turned, and Nell followed. They made their way through the crowd of milling people talking with each other. The die was cast. She was more like him than them. Always had been, always would be.

*

Late Sunday afternoon, Nell sat at the kitchen table, pencil in hand. The letter was finished. She folded it carefully, placed it in an envelope and sealed it. On the front of the envelope, she copied the address written in her father's fine script on the worn out scrap of paper. She studied it and sighed.

It read: Nola Songbird Mennebar and Jason Mennebar, Rural Route 17, Dunbar, Illinois.

Maybe, just maybe, this was the name and address of the woman and man whose child he'd stolen. Monday morning, she drove into town and mailed the letter.

*

A few days later, the man was back. Dressed in black, he stood by his black horse up on the knoll, watching the farm, looking like a coal-black, menacing shadow. She latched the hen house door and walked slowly to the house, watching him all the way. She carried the basket of eggs inside, washed and dried them, and placed them in the cooler to chill. Then she went back outside. She crossed the yard to the barn before she glanced up at the knoll. He was still up there. He stood there a long time while she ignored him and went about her business. Later, when she looked up again, he was gone.

She drove to town and worked with Margaret, making new dresses. She attended church on Sundays. She walked and slept and ate and lived, while each day Addition Jones watched her from the knoll. Sometimes he sat under the huge oak tree. Sometimes he leaned against it, disappearing like an illusion when other people came out to the farm.

Sometimes the stress of holding the secret position of companionship with him made her half crazy, but she held steady and waited. Life hadn't been easy so far. *Why would that change now?* She asked herself. *Man trouble. Why did God do this to me? Always a man.* Yet she'd never had one look her way, she'd never slept with one, and she was innocent of causing even one of the male species trouble.

But she'd lived with a cruel father and learned well how to wait to see what a man might do next, so she would know what she must do next. All she knew about was one alcoholic man. Maybe the dark man wasn't an alcoholic. If he wasn't, she didn't know what to expect. She went on with her life. It looked normal and simple. No one knew it now included both the sweetness and horror of a steadily building, unexplored bond between the two outcasts.

Summer dragged on. At last Nell couldn't stand the stress; something needed to give. She dressed for church Sunday morning, walked outside and looked up at the familiar sight of the dark man on the knoll. She could imagine his black eyes, filled with rage, boring into hers. Well, she just wasn't going to take any more. Not today. Maybe tomorrow, but not today.

She waited until she was sure his attention was on her before she walked into the barn. She unlocked the door to his old room for the first time since she moved in. She propped the door open. She laid the key to the padlock by the open door for him to see, and walked back out into the middle of the yard. She swept her arms out wide in an invitation for him to come down to the barn, then she climbed into the buggy and left.

She went home with Claude and Margaret after church. They ate dinner. She got home in the late afternoon. She took care of the horse and buggy before she went to the back of the barn. The door to his room was closed and locked. The key to the padlock was gone. Everything else looked the same. She sighed. At least it was out in the open. He'd owned who he was. What she was doing felt dangerous, but she felt forced to follow where she was led.

*

One morning a few days later, Nell was weeding sweet peas in the flowerbed by the house when a fine black buggy wheeled smartly into the yard. She stood and watched a tall, swarthy older man dressed in black step down from the buggy. He turned and helped a small, dove-like woman dressed in black out of the buggy, then placed his arm protectively around her shoulders. They walked towards Nell.

Nell stared at the shock of pure white hair falling straight across the man's forehead and instantly knew who he was. She looked at him, then up to the knoll. Addition Jones was still up there. Her heart pounded with excitement.

The man standing up on the knoll was a younger image of the man standing in front of her!

"Are you Nell? We just received your letter. We've been away. We came as soon as we could. I'm Jason Mennebar, and this is my wife, Nola Songbird Mennebar."

It was too much for Nell. Her hands flew to her chest. She tried to speak, but no words came out. Instead, she gasped and looked up at the knoll, then back at them.

The couple's eyes followed hers, and the three of them stared up at the knoll. The dark man stood under the oak tree, lounging against it, while below him stood the mother and father of a lost child and the daughter of the evil man who had robbed them of that child. A sob escaped the woman's mouth.

"Is that Alexander?"

She moaned and staggered a step forward, her hands stretched out towards the knoll. Jason pulled her back into the protective custody of his arms. To Nell, it seemed to take forever before Jason dropped his arms from around his wife and took a hesitant step towards the knoll and his son.

*

To Jason Mennebar, the distance between them meant nothing. The years of yearning fell away. Now only physical distance remained before he could at last reclaim his son. He took another small, cautious step forward. A soft noise escaped his throat, and he heard the voices of his ancestors speaking their Traveler's words.

"Our son! Our son! Our own true blood!" they chanted, as they called out through him to the man on the hill. But the fate his ancestors had suffered flew across his mind, making him hesitate. They were fated to traveling forever, to searching for the Lost One and never finding Him. His only son was such a Lost One. But he too, like the rest of his clan, would never give up the search.

His soul quickened with fear and hope. He took another step forward, staring up at the knoll, watching his son intently. Nola moaned. Nell embraced her and pulled her close against her side. The two women swayed back and forth while Jason crossed the yard at a snail's pace. Slowly he started climbing the hill towards the man staring down at him.

Jason watched as his son finally realized something was wrong. He grabbed his horse's reins in his hands and prepared to mount. Nell sucked in her breath and held it. He was going to ride away and leave them again! She clutched Nola tighter to her side.

The rider must have been drawn to something about the man climbing the hill, because he waited until Jason topped the hill before he mounted his horse. He sat his horse while it danced around, ready to spring into motion as Jason appeared.

The two men stared at each other. They were mirrors of each other. Exactly alike except for their ages. Father and son. Jason threw out his arms and claimed the rider with one longing shout.

"My son!"

His shout, full of compassion and love and joy, flew out of him. He watched helplessly as a look of natural recognition of their shared genetics crossed his son's face before disbelief and horror followed it.

His son recoiled from him. He jerked his horse around. The big black horse fled down the path. Jason stared hungrily after his son until he was out of sight.

He turned and made his way back down the hill and across the yard to Nola. He grabbed her and held her like she was made of spun glass. He spoke soothing words to her in a language Nell didn't understand. The words he spoke felt as old as time. Then he looked over Nola's bowed head at Nell.

"It's him, all right!" he said grimly, his mouth a tight, trembling white line. "He's a Mennebar! You've found us our son after all these years!"

Nell grabbed at Nola again, and Jason let her go. He trailed them as they wound their way to the porch steps. Cautiously, he stayed a few steps behind. He'd weathered the intense emotional storms of the women of his culture many times and learned early on to stay out of the path of their emotional tornados.

Women! Always feeling too strong about everything while us men have to stay practical, do the thinking, and straighten things out! He thought, as he followed them up the steps, across the porch, and into the house.

Nell led the way into the kitchen and stopped. Jason led them to the kitchen table, pushed them gently down into chairs, found lemonade and poured glasses for all of them.

"The things you said in your letter were true, yes?"

Nell nodded.

"Tell us what happened!" he demanded. Nell told them all she knew. Jason paced the floor in rage at the evils Nell's father did to all of them. Nola put her head in her hands and sobbed.

"It's all my fault! I should never have looked at that evil man. But I did, and I left Alexander all alone in the basket! It's all my fault!"

Nell stared at Nola's bent head and at Jason holding her, comforting her.

"It's not your fault. My father was the criminal. He did it, not you!" she wailed and burst into tears.

Jason shook his head at both of them and shouted, "Stop it! All is not lost! Alexander is alive, he appears to be healthy—certainly, he's all grown up. It's got to be enough for now. Either way, stop this damn wailing! What's done is done! Let's all go forward and see what we can salvage from the losses we've taken. Let's try to find the man our lost child has become before you drown in your crying or we get too damn old and die! He'll be dead and gone before you women stop your moaning about him! Save your crying for something else!"

*

Jason and Nola stayed with Nell as long as they could. With unspoken agreement, they went through each day taking turns watching the knoll above the house. They agreed it was best no one know they were there for the time being. They tended the farm when Nell went into town. The three of them ate and slept where they could watch the knoll. But he never came back.

Jason and Nola were forced to leave. Their large farm needed tending; their hired man would not be able to keep up with it much

114

longer. They left with hope in their hearts. Alexander was alive. Jason had almost laid hands on his son. Nell knew they wouldn't let him get lost again. They planned to hire a detective to find him. They hugged Nell when they left with a promise to let each other know as soon as they saw him again.

*

She stood in the yard, holding an official eviction notice. Thirty days to get off the farm. She looked around in despair. What would she do with the animals and the garden? She would have to find a new place to live. To do that, she would need help. She would have to tell Margaret her secret. Quickly she hitched up the buggy and drove to town.

"Margaret, I need you to help me find another place to live!"

Nell wrung her hands together.

"I need your help, and I haven't told you everything."

She told her story.

"...and he kept coming back and watching me from the knoll, and now he's served an eviction notice on me!"

She didn't mention the letter or the visit from the Mennebars, or that she knew his real

115

name now. Alexander Mennebar, a name she repeated to herself every day.

*

Nell stood out front, shading her eyes, studying the neglected, run-down boarding house on the edge of town. She eyed the deep, shady porch embracing the front and sides, and the wide, inviting steps. She looked up at the second story windows framed with fancy gingerbread trim.

"Someone once dreamed big for this place!" she thought.

*

The little yellow house was empty. Everything had been loaded into buckboards and taken to the boarding house in town. Everyone in town argued about what was right.

"She shouldn't have fixed that cursed farm up!" some said. Others said, "It's just like that man to find a way to take it away from her!"

The fact he was alive didn't improve their opinions of him. They became even more suspicious when Addition Jones transferred a lot of money into the town bank.

"Where'd he get it from?" they asked each other.

"It has to be tainted money for him to have it!"

They voiced their opinions freely to Nell. She listened wearily, but didn't respond. They came out to the farm and took the animals away and picked all the vegetables out of the garden. They took the feed and hay and all the farm equipment. The barns, sheds, and the cold house stood stripped and bare. The last things to go were the two rocking chairs on the front porch. Nell carried them to town herself and placed them on the boarding house porch. Addition Jones' farm was bare bones once more.

Nell drove out to the farm one last time to say goodbye. She didn't tell anyone where she was going. She wanted to be alone so she could think things out. Everything happened so fast, and it took a lot of work. She was deathly tired of the constant voices of people and from having too much to do. She was tired of listening to people's opinions. They were good people, but she couldn't stand any more for now.

She drove the buggy into the quiet yard and stopped. She drew in a deep breath of the flower-scented air and looked up at the knoll above the house. The huge oak tree was shady and inviting, but no one stood or sat under it. She climbed out of the buggy and wandered around the yard. She inspected the flowers blooming in the neat beds in front of the house. Some of the women wanted to pull them up so he couldn't have them. Their meanness made her feel strange inside, and she ordered them to leave the flowers alone. She told herself the blooms had a right to their lives while they lasted.

Sudden anger rushed through her. Besides, the flowers wouldn't live long, because she couldn't imagine him keeping a garden or allowing flowers to grow. If he so much as walked past one, it would shrivel up and die! And no doubt, he wouldn't care anything about having sun scented sheets on his bed, the beast!

She pictured him in the house, alone in his bed. He would be fully dressed in black, laying there, frowning up at the ceiling. She pictured bare walls, bare floors, and gray utility mats at the front and back doors. She pictured a bare pantry and the dark, forbidding ugliness he would make of the house she'd built.

The long-held, righteous anger helping her get through the move deserted her. She stumbled over to the porch and thumped down. She was so damn tired of the town hating him! Yes, now she was one of the many causes they hated him for, but she just wanted it to stop! Every time she heard another thing against him, she shriveled up a little more inside.

The stories about his growing up grew bigger and worse with each telling. For her, justice was finally served. He could have the house, to hell with him! She built it for him in gratitude for being her only companion, and in redemption for her father's sins against him. But trying to stop the townspeople from spreading cruel lies about him was like trying to stop a damned up wildfire.

She was alone again. She never wanted anyone to know about the secret hope she'd harbored; for now, they were forced to hate each other. It was expected. The town wouldn't have it any other way. He had done something wrong again; they felt smug and vindicated; they felt righteous about ignoring him when he was growing up, and about believing he was a murderer when he wasn't.

In the public telling of her father's kidnapping of him, she cleared him of the murders everyone wanted to believe he committed. Now he could come home to his new house, his clean farm. Justice was served, but the yearning she didn't dare name, the secret hope she'd fought to keep, was gone. The dream of any kind of love between them was too late. It was too tender, too new, and too young. It had been smashed down by the trampling feet and wagging tongues swarming all over this farm the last few weeks.

For a time, hope had danced alone atop a burned-out shell of a house, defying an evil man's dying words, starting a new meaning with wood, walls, and stone. Now the hope that once was hers belonged to him, soft and yellow and new. She had provided it for him, using her father's money, as was just and appropriate. It was over. It was time to dream a new dream.

A long time passed before she was cried out. She felt like a wrung-out dishrag. A dull, hopeless feeling settled into a hard knot beneath her heart. She would keep her secret locked up and let it die off as it needed to. She couldn't afford to keep it alive, justice or no justice. It hurt too much. She climbed in the buggy and drove slowly back to town.

Chapter 8. Wearing Black

Intersections
Intervals

Addition Jones stared out the window at the cherry trees rowing the elegant Chicago street below, watching the fashionable, laughing people strolling beneath the pink blossoms filling the tops of the trees. A bitter smile chiseled his mouth into a curve. He dropped the heavy red velvet drape back in place, pulled an ornate gold watch from his pocket, opened it and looked at the time. He snapped the watch shut and stared down at the shiny gold circle in his hand. His heavy black brows furrowed into a frown. He could see his reflection in the golden orb.

Automatically, he reached up to smooth back the unruly shock of stubborn, straight black hair hanging over his brow before he glanced into the large, ornate mirror across the room.

His crisp white shirt was immaculate, as usual. His cravat was perfectly tied. He grimaced as he tugged a black dress coat from its hanger and shrugged into it. He looked at himself in the mirror again. He always wore black, though it never seemed to hang quite right on him. Regardless, he wore it immaculately, in his opinion. It was his trademark, his own personal brand among his business associates and among the ladies casting yearning glances his way. None of them ever dared ask him why he always wore black. They would never know it was for his perpetual mourning and a deep desire for respect. That was his damn business.

He meant business, and they knew it instantly upon meeting him. He never needed to say it. His fierce hawk face and the look of his large-framed, long body clad in black, spoke volumes for him.

He let out a heavy breath and frowned. He was tired of the rounds of meetings and social gatherings where people stared at him, then looked away because of his power, his looks, and his money.

He assessed himself. His speech was adequate, but by nature he kept it sparse. He was educated in matters of the world, and through the most grueling work, had moved up from a hobo's existence to this fashionable mansion, never touching the Smith's money on the way. He was a self-made man. He had hired the best tutors to educate him. There was nothing more he needed. Yet, with his unerring instinct, he knew that lately, something more than being bored and tired of his life was bothering him.

He let himself out of the house and braced himself for the fashionable, absolutely boring evening ahead. During the evening, his mind restlessly chased shadows of mystery and money in spite of his concentration on the music and dinner. He left early without an explanation to anyone. He never explained himself. The people who knew him were used to it, and though they disliked his rude manners, they said nothing to him about his abrupt and aggressive nature; they whispered avidly among themselves when he wasn't around, avoiding confronting him directly.

Back home, he went straight to bed with one of his rare headaches. They were becoming more frequent lately. He understood that he had a violent nature and he knew suppressing it was the cause of his headaches.

Late that night, he woke with a start. The headache was gone. He'd dreamed about the Smith farm again. Until recently, he ignored his dreams of the farm. He never walked the land or touched it or felt anything. Everything was always at a distance. He floated above and around it.

But lately, his dreams of the farm were different. He walked the land in them now. He touched it and crumbled dirt in his hands and relived portions of the pain, loneliness, and bitterness that filled his early life. He relived the isolation and loneliness and the darkness and the horrible needs that never got met. He relived the layering of the resentments he placed around his heart to survive.

He'd made one friend back in those days, and that friend walked away from him. No one would ever get close to him again! He'd survived the nightmare of his childhood and youth. Those days were in the past, and he intended to keep them there.

He stared up into the blackness of his elegant bedroom. He was damn tired of being dogged by dreams of that place. Suddenly he realized what he needed to do. He would put it behind him for good. He would go back to the farm, something he vowed never to do. *Well, I should have done it long ago,* he told himself. The burnt-out shell of a farmhouse needed to be razed, the buildings destroyed, and the land sold. *No doubt I will find solace then.* His decision made, he sighed, closed his eyes and fell into a restless sleep.

The next day, he gave his solicitors instructions, arranged room and board for himself and his horse Midnight in Benton, a small town near Cross Grove, and boarded the train.

He never wanted to see anyone in Cross Grove again. He didn't intend for any of them to know he still existed or ever came back to the farm. It was none of their damn business.

Early morning found him riding Midnight towards the farm with his camping gear tied behind Midnight's saddle. They suited each other perfectly, for Midnight was long, rangy and ink black, with a compelling temperament that could only be quelled by his owner. He was a one-man horse.

While he rode, he made plans for the disposal of the farm. He would bring in people from outside to tear down every building on the place and burn them down to black ashes. He pictured the ashes blowing away in the wind and grinned sardonically. Then he would have the land scraped clean of the remains of the charred house and have it removed from the property. Maybe that would release the curse from the farm. *I will stay just long enough to oversee the job, to make sure it is done exactly the way I want. Then I will sell the place,* he thought.

He stopped to set up camp by the familiar, thin, singing creek running across an outer edge of the farm. In a short time, he surveyed his camp. The tent was up, the fire pit loaded with kindling. Midnight was grazing contentedly nearby. He ate before he saddled Midnight and rode slowly across the farm, the two of them moving like one large shadow. His farm. Wild and abandoned, the fields were filled with high weeds, stalky wildflowers, and trees. The scent of them stole pleasantly across his senses. He stopped to watch a wild hare bolt across a dandelion-filled meadow. Birdsong trilled in the quiet air, and he felt the tendrils of a warm peace begin to curl through his belly. Surprised, he supposed he had every right to be peaceful on his own land.

His eyes roamed the land as he rode. He'd explored every inch of this farm as a child and young man, and true to his intense nature and needs, he'd made it his. He rode through the familiar fields, recognizing everything, trying to stay cold and neutral to the land he'd raised himself on.

He'd fled this place as a scared young man. Slowly, he began to realize how much the fields and animals once meant to him. He recalled his surprised, delighted laughter as a young boy when a sparrow's wings brushed past him in flight after he startled it in a hedgerow, and how good the animals tasted after he learned to trap and clean and cook them.

Back then he was always hungry. He thought about how he was forced to harden against everything except the land and animals that surrounded him after the Smiths made him move out to the barn.

You were all I had. You kept me alive, he admitted silently to the life surrounding him. He remembered the feel of the brown rabbits he held in his arms, and the smooth feathered birds he contained in rudely made cages until he could stand to let them fly away again.

His need to destroy the farm was still battling with his memories when he topped the knoll above the farmhouse, expecting to see blackened, charred ruins below. He jerked Midnight to a stop and exclaimed in surprise.

"What the hell?"

His black eyes narrowed in amazement and fury. The Smith house was gone! Instead of charred ruins and devastation, a charming one story, yellow wood house stood primly below, exactly where the charred remains of the burned out old house once stood! Frozen in shock and rage, he sat perfectly still, searching out everything with his eyes.

The land around the cheerful little house was smooth and clean. Flowers and a vegetable garden grew nearby. His black eyes raked coldly across the shiny windows, the white porch with wide, welcoming steps, the neat, bright flowerbeds banking the house, and the green lawn.

He looked at the barn. Renewed with crisp, apple red paint and new wood. Other improvements, ones he'd never thought of. He admitted to himself that they were clever. There were new sheds and a smokehouse. He inspected the farm over and over again with his eyes. There was no sign of the ravaged, empty farm he expected to find. Everything was new, and it looked like whoever did this moved in recently.

Rage raced through him. A squatter built a house on his property without his permission! Worse, they built over the ashes of the old house!

Well, they will lose their investment!, he thought grimly, dancing Midnight in a circle. He would see to it!

Just then, a tall, thin woman with hair pulled back in a bun came out of the house. An old woman. She didn't see him at first. He watched her feed chickens and gather eggs. He didn't see anyone else. He knew the instant she realized he was there, for her body stiffened and she hurried back to the house.

If she's smart, she'll have a gun somewhere, he thought, turning Midnight from the knoll and riding away.

He camped by the small creek and spent his days on the knoll above the farm, watching the old woman working his land. He sat or stood under the tree, watching her with anger and other feelings he couldn't and didn't want to name. The images of the old house that once stood there and the hate, hunger, and isolation he remembered warred daily with the tranquil, happy scene below him.

It was his place to destroy, to change the farm, not hers! Yet he had dreaded it. The fact that it was over gave him both relief and anger.

He didn't know what to do. At night, he sat by his campfire, staring into the flames, wondering what the hell he was up to. He didn't know why he didn't put in motion papers to legally evict her as soon as he discovered her on his property. He didn't know why he chose, instead, to haunt her from atop the knoll.

He knew she was scared of him. He could see it in her actions. He shook his head at himself. It got worse. He'd gone farther. He'd met her on the road on purpose on a sunny Sunday morning. He knew her habits well enough by then to know she was on her way to church when he'd waylaid her. She'd stopped her buggy on the path and sat staring down at his farm with a peaceful, contented look on her face. That's when he decided to let her know the farm was still his, that he could throw her off it any time he wanted to.

He rode Midnight close to her buggy and stopped, surprised. Another shock. He was wrong. She wasn't an old woman. She was somewhere in middle age. She sat perfectly still and stared at him with a thinned down, wide mouth and large, gray eyes the color of the doves he watched and heard cooing to him through the windows of his Chicago office, causing him to yearn for the freedom of an open field.

She was not at all what he expected. His eyes raked over her, looking for something he could feel contempt for. He noted that her dress fit her long, rangy figure perfectly. The bonnet she wore was modern and stylish.

He'd glared at her with eyes full of contrived contempt and hate, expecting her to drop her cool, thoughtful eyes from his like everybody else did. But she held his look without hate or fear. Most people couldn't hold it at all. Did he imagine the tiny bit of longing in her eyes, a longing familiar to him, a tendril of something lost and never found, touching a place in him long hidden from the world?

The frozen silence grew deafening. He finally jerked Midnight away. He found himself riding jauntily down to the farm and through the yard and around all the buildings while she watched. Then he rode back up the knoll, past her and out of sight. He didn't know what else to do.

After their silent confront, the game between them escalated. He didn't know what might have happened or how long it would have lasted, except for those blasted people showing up. That day, he'd felt intensely dangerous, waiting for any chance to vent his anger on someone over his confusion, his shame, his wretched need to watch the woman every day. He would have done something bad that day— he didn't know what—but the old man clawed his way to the top of the hill, putting a stop to everything he'd ever known.

His remembered his heart racing madly as he watched the man and woman climb out of their buggy. Regardless of them, it was time for his madness to stop. He stood his ground and didn't hide. He waited while the old man climbed the hill, not knowing what he would do to him. He would never forget the faces of the two women below, staring up at him while he waited to destroy, to maim or kill. Their yearning, white faces were etched forever in his mind.

Finally he realized he was temporarily insane, and if he stayed on foot, he would surely kill or hurt one or all of them. He mounted Midnight and waited for the old man.

Midnight danced on top of the knoll while bitter words boiled like bile in the back of his throat. But when the old man topped the hill and he saw an older version of his himself mirrored back to him, his rage instantly cooled into confused shock.

"My son!" the old man shouted joyfully, opening his arms wide. Astounded, he'd almost swooned at the word the man claimed him with.

"Son!"

They stared at each other, both dressed in black with the same shock of hair falling over their foreheads, mirroring the same steely black eyes, hawk noses, and chiseled lips set in swarthy, dark skin. In self-defense against the shock shattering through him, he turned Midnight and ran. Back at camp, he stared into the fire's dancing shadows. He didn't understand any of it. It was time for him to leave. He would break camp in the morning.

*

He moved back into his familiar world as if nothing ever happened and immediately ordered his lawyer to evict the woman from his farm.

He stood in front of the mirror, adjusting his tie. He knew her name now. Nell Miller. She was off his land. He should have been the one to resurrect his farm, not some rangy, tall old maid! The eviction should have been enough, but every night he still dreamed of the farm and the dark face so like his own, a face filled with agonizing concern for him, and of the two women below who stared longingly up at him, one bearing the gray eyes of a dove.

What did they want from him? There was nothing to give them. His dreams were getting worse. He needed to do something. There was a curse on his soul, calling him back to the nightmare home he once fled.

At last he gave in. He would go back once more. This time, he would stay just long

132

enough to supervise the destruction of the new buildings on the farm. He would level everything on it and sell the place. Simple. Surely the nightmares would stop then.

He made arrangements with the same hotel in Benton for the first night of his stay. He planned to move into the empty yellow house the next day and stay there until he was ready to burn it to the ground.

He moved back to the farm and into the little yellow house. Grimly, he rode into Cross Grove and watched the shock and hate come over the surprised faces of the townspeople.

He became a part of Cross Grove again. He knew he was a hated citizen and always would be. He would only bother the town for his needs, not socialize in any way. He made lists of what he needed, keeping his rides into Cross Grove short and quick.

Out on the farm, he searched for boards, ashes, anything from the old house, any reminders of the bitter days he'd survived. There were none. He sat on the front porch and stared at the empty, newly-painted barn.

He thought about his little room in the barn. He'd locked it and kept the key in his pocket since the Sunday she invited him down to the farm. But he couldn't bring himself to open the door of his little room just yet. Too many painful memories were stored in it. They would make him feel, and he didn't want to feel any more than he was having to right now. He knew he was living in his own emotional version of overload, and that was enough.

"Damn!" he muttered to himself. Gone was the powerful, planned, peaceful, moneyed existence he'd scrabbled so hard for, one allowing only the problems he wanted into his world. His carefully laid plans for a rich, insulated life were shot to hell, tangled in the unexpected surprises that seemed to be awaiting him at each turn of his existence these days.

He strode through the fields, pulling up weeds and wildflowers and tossing them in the air. He wandered through the new buildings and across the land, alternating between the need to stay connected to the only things that once mattered to him, fighting his primal need to destroy something.

He stayed exhausted, angry, and confused. His mixed feelings held constant sway over him. The townspeople felt the coldness coming from him whenever they encountered him. He froze them out with the scarecrow way he looked, in spite of his expensive clothes.

He rode to Benton and hired a handful of workers. They bunked in the barn and returned to Benton on weekends. The work he assigned them was sporadic; he kept changing his mind. The men did their jobs over and over. They repainted the sheds and barn. They mowed the tall grass in the fields and plowed others. They cleaned out fence rows and deepened the well.

He told himself and them, that he was just improving the farm so he would get a better price when he sold it. At last he gave up the pretense and sent them home. He just wasn't up to burning the place down, no matter how hard he tried. It was time to make new decisions.

Chapter 9. Homecoming

Square One
Bone Stew

Dressed in his Sunday best, he stepped out of the little yellow house, black hat in hand, and looked around. The sheds had been torn down and rebuilt. They were now so sturdy, nothing could bring them down short of an earthquake or tornado. The barn had four new coats of paint. The well was so deep it probably reached close to China.

He sighed. And still, he wasn't able to bring himself to destroy the place. Or leave it. Or sell it. Or rent it out. It was all his, for better or worse. It took a hell of a long time, but his cursed ambivalence was at last gone. He'd finally accepted his Fate; he was stuck here for now.

He mounted Midnight, leaned over and patted his neck, grinning at his thoughts. He felt lighter than he had in a long time. It was a perfectly lovely morning to do what he planned. Since he was forced to stay on the farm for the time being, he might as well give the folks in town a little treat. Why shouldn't they suffer too? He would go to Sunday church meeting dressed in the expensive clothes they expected him to wear. He was back, but with money and power now, and he certainly wouldn't want to disappoint all those fine folks who believed he'd burned the Smiths up in their beds!

He wanted and needed all of them to be shocked. He wanted all the people who ignored his existence for all those years to pay attention. He wanted them to know he was back, and they were going to suffer for it, like he suffered for years because of their foul silence in the face of the Smith's blatant cruelty to him. Yes, church, where they all acted holier than thou, where they thought only their goodness was seen by God, was a fine place to start. Their own personal devil was going to show up and bring their sins inside their sanctuary, sit down in their midst, and stay just as long as he wanted.

*

Nell sat in a pew near the back. Her hands lay spare and empty in her lap. Absently, she listened to the sermon. She was thinking about Addition Jones. He was improving the farm. Was he planning to stay?

She listened to the gossip, then changed the subject as soon as she could. Her attempt at the redemption of Addition Jones was over. She'd moved on. The boarding house was working out well as a combination dress shop and a home for her.

Her contented daydreams were interrupted when she heard someone come in and sit down in the back. They were late. Absently, she glanced around with a half smile. Her mind froze in surprise as she watched Addition Jones sit down in the last pew. He sat ramrod straight in the empty pew and fixed an angry glare on the preacher's face.

She jerked her head back around and stared at the preacher. She watched the preacher's lips move but couldn't hear his words over the thunder of her heart. She began to sweat in the cool morning air pouring through the open windows and doors. The church was too hot. She felt like she was smothering. Other people were turning around and staring at him. Voices whispered, but he sat like a large obsidian statue, oblivious to everyone around him.

At last, the preacher brought his sermon to a close. Everyone stood up and sang the last hymn. The minister stepped down from the pulpit and strode to the back of the church where Addition Jones stood. The preacher shook his hand and spoke to him, but Nell didn't hear anything he said.

She stared at Addition Jones. How strange! His Adam's apple was working up and down like the farmer who bought her old farm. She'd heard that Adam's apple bobbing was a sign of emotional nervousness in a man. What did he have to be nervous about? She was surprised at the idea he might feel emotional distress over anything. Quickly she broke the tiny thread of sympathy she was weaving for him. She was mistaken!

He turned away and strode out the door. He was standing by his horse when she stepped outside. He didn't seem to be in any hurry to leave. The congregation poured out of the church. They didn't stand around and talk and joke with each other like they usually did. They shook the preacher's hand and scurried away, like leaves flying away in a brisk wind.

Nell stood by the steps, watching him. Everyone was gone before she made up her mind to speak to him. She marched purposefully over to him. He looked at her and twirled his hat brim in his fingers. She waited for him to speak, but he seemed content to stand there forever, not saying a word, just watching her. Exasperated, she took a deep breath

"I'm Nell Miller, and you are Addition Jones."

She braced herself for the onslaught of anger her words would bring. Their eyes locked, and he snorted in a very ungentlemanly way. His black eyes shot daggers into her clear gray eyes.

"Why did you build a house on my land?"

He frowned down at her, waiting for an answer. He was taller than she was. Most men weren't. A tiny pulse of fear began in her throat as her mind put two and two together. This man didn't talk to folks around here. Maybe he didn't know the story behind her move to his farm. Maybe he only saw her as a squatter on his land.

She couldn't get any words out. The weight of him felt like a giant boulder. He filled up the space around her. She tried to swallow. He didn't know! Now was not the time to confess. She looked around desperately. No one else was around. She didn't want to be near him when he found out. Anger rushed through her. Nobody else in town would tell him. They gossiped instead, leaving it up to her.

He turned away, mounted his horse and rode off without a backward glance. She tottered to the church steps in relief and horror. It was only right he know the truth. And she would have to be the one to tell him, because it was her father who kidnapped him.

Anger rose in her, swift and sharp. It wasn't fair! Well, she simply wouldn't do it! She jumped up and hurried home. She ran up the wide steps and slammed through the front door of the boardinghouse. Her eyes scanned the rooms, searching for something to work at.

With stony determination, she rolled up her sleeves. Busy day followed busy day. She worked until she fell into bed at night, exhausted. She jumped out of bed and began again the next morning.

But a day finally came when there was nothing left to do. The yard was smooth and green. Flower beds dotted the walkway to the boarding house. The porch was shiny with fresh green paint and scrolled white railing. Everything inside the boardinghouse was washed or painted or rehung or renailed or starched within an inch of its life.

She was exhausted. She wandered outside and sat down beneath the oak tree shading the front porch. Her eyelids drooped. She leaned back against the old tree and dozed off.

A short time later, she jerked out of her nap with a start, her gray eyes wide. The Mennebars! How could she forget them? A detective was searching for him! What if they heard he was back on the farm? What if they went to see him before he knew what her father did to him?

She didn't write to them as she promised. Guilt washed over her. It was time to tell him and write to the Mennebars before anything else happened. She jumped up and ran in the house.

A short time later, she whirled her buggy into his yard and stopped. Dust curled through the air around her. She looked around. The farm looked deserted. She felt the heaviness in the still air and it slowed her down. She sighed with sadness and trepidation. Grimly she pinned her windblown hair back into the bun on top of her head, and climbed out of the buggy. The house looked small and empty without the welcoming rocking chairs sitting on the porch.

She crossed the yard and stomped up the wide porch steps. She knocked on the door, stepped back, and waited. She turned around when she heard the barn door open. He stood there, watching her, waiting. She walked down the steps and grudgingly trudged towards him, her stomach knotting with urgency and fear. He didn't move. His hard, stoic face held no sign of welcome. It was the face of a man enduring an unpleasant, unwelcome visit.

She studied him warily as she worked her way across the yard. He was a rugged, earthy man. He didn't carry the easy stance of youth, but rather the measured stance of an older man accustomed to being in charge. The beginnings of silver wings at his temples were striking against his midnight black hair.

Abruptly, a new thought crossed her mind. Would he murder her as soon as she told him what her father did to him? Maybe. She turned and headed back to her buggy and climbed in.

She looked at him. He didn't move or speak. She drove the buggy as close to him as she dared, and stopped. It was his right to know.

Suddenly she sensed that the dark fates they'd each endured all their lives were watching, waiting to see how this turned out. New life would either end or go forward for both of them from this moment on, for better or worse.

She sat in the buggy, ready to take flight. Gasping, she reached inside herself, grabbing the hasty, cruel, waiting words of confession, throwing them at him.

"Addition Jones, there's something you don't know."

He waited, grim and silent. She took a deep breath and went at the news sideways, trying to soften the blow.

"My father was an evil man. He was a mean and crazy drunkard. He died a while back. On his deathbed, he confessed a crime to me. He said that years ago he fell in love with a woman who wouldn't have him when she found out he was married.

She turned him away and married somebody else real quick and they had a baby. You were that baby. My father kidnapped you to spite your mother, and he left you on the steps of this farm. Your parents searched for you and the kidnapper, but they never found either one of you. But that's not all.

After a few years, my father said he decided to find you and return you to your mother. He said when he found you, you were grown up. He couldn't take you back to your mother, so he set fire to your house and left. You didn't murder the Smith's. He did.

After he died, I came to Cross Grove to tell you what he did, but you were gone. I told the people in town what my father did to you, and they know the truth now. That was owed to you. Then I built the house and waited to see if you would come back, and you did. That's all."

She watched his face change from a cold, silent mask to one of surprised, hurt fury. His intense black eyes searched her face for any secrets she might be holding back from her confession. She would have hated to try to keep anything back from this man. Suddenly, the fury drained from his eyes, and they became unreadable.

She stared at him in surprise. The cold, smooth mask he'd worn earlier slid back over his face. He didn't look surprised, excited, or anything different than before she revealed the terrible truth to him.

In a hard, careless voice he said, "I want the rocking chairs brought back. They belong on this porch."

She was stunned. Didn't he understand what she'd told him?

"What?"

He wanted the damned rocking chairs back? She shook her head in disbelief. What if her father never confessed on his deathbed? What if she was the kind of person who didn't give a damn about rectifying her father's wrongs? All the work and money she'd spent on this farm meant nothing to him? The sweat and labor her friends and neighbors poured into this place in unspoken redemption didn't matter a damn to him? He just wanted the rocking chairs back?

He wasn't making any sense, and that scared her. Nell jerked the reins hard and wheeled the buggy out of the yard as fast as she could. She felt sick to her stomach. She did the right thing. She told the town, and now him. Her duty to him was over!

She climbed the steps to the boardinghouse and went inside. She was exhausted. She locked the door, pulled down the shades and crawled into bed. Tears started and didn't stop for days. They dried up and she fell into a deep well of despair. She did the necessary chores and nothing more. She kept her secret from Margaret, but it left her alone again with no one to turn to. Well, she told herself, she was used to it. She'd endured a lifetime of it before she came here!

She told Margaret and the other ladies that she was a little under the weather. Maybe she was working too hard lately and needed to take a little rest. They clucked in sympathy and left her alone.

Underneath the lie, lit fires of icy rage consumed her. She trembled with outrage. She wanted to destroy both her father and Addition Jones. All of her life she'd believed in the goodness of people. She excused her father by believing it was the drink and his weak, vain personality keeping him a prisoner of his own meanness. Now she knew better. He liked courting his cruelties and enjoyed the practice of refining them. He never suffered like she once believed. He was completely selfish. All that mattered to him was his own wants and needs; everything in his world existed only to serve him.

Then that lying, cheating devil burdened her with Addition Jones with his dying breath! Bet he was in Hell, laughing! Two selfish, mean, cruel, violent men, neither giving a damn about anybody else!

Too bad he died not knowing he'd dropped Addition Jones into a world where he was forced to become exactly like himself!

Now he had a living partner in crime, for the legacy of hate was passed through him successfully to Addition Jones. She'd been forced to endure her father; she didn't have a choice, but she didn't have to put up with Addition Jones!

Nell's dark thoughts and anger never ceased. There was no one to tell about her loss of hope and disappointment. When she was young, when her life force weakened from too much loneliness and no companionship, Angels, the kind she read about in her Bible, Nature and the animals around her, came and helped her survive.

Now she realized it was her mother's choice to stay weak and defenseless in the face of evil. She'd sickened and died from it, helpless and praying to the end for the redemption of her husband, instead of taking her daughter and going home to her parent's farm like anyone in their right mind would have done. Instead, she'd let him destroy her.

She was a second place love, a servant to the self-sacrificing ways of her mother. She'd grown up old and alone, a gray-haired child-spinster sitting in a swing no human ever pushed, waiting dutifully to listen to her mother's whining or her father's loud, angry rages.

Nell gave up hope and accepted her fate. For the rest of her life, the best in her soul would remain un-companioned. It was her fate, her destiny. And, it was safer that way, much safer than getting caught in the kind of marriage her parents lived and died in.

*

One morning she lay in bed, waiting for the familiar darkness to overcome her. She listened to the ticking clock and searched with her mind through the empty room for the dark thoughts stalking her every waking moment the past few weeks. There was nothing left but emptiness. No good or bad, just emptiness.

She lay like a stone, letting the rosy peace of emptiness and the energy acceptance gives seep into her soul. After a while, she crawled out of bed and looked around. Her clothes needed washing. Thick layers of dust covered everything.

She yawned and stretched. Instinctively, she knew she'd survived an old poison dwelling in her soul. She'd survived her own dark night of the soul. Her belief in goodness was small, but still burning.

She heard the sound of laughing girls running past her. The sound lasted just an instant. They were counting on her for something, but she didn't know what it was.

Nell shook her head. There was a lot in this old world far beyond understanding, and she didn't have time to ponder it right now. She wrinkled her nose. She needed a bath! She'd worn the same clothes for days. She looked in the mirror. Her hair was greasy. She made coffee and ate. Then she cleaned up and started wash water to boiling.

The next morning, she raised the shades over the front windows. The house was clean and in order again, and so was she. It was time to go forward. Time to visit Margaret. She didn't want to be alone any more. She no longer wanted to work from daylight 'til dark on any damn farm or at dressmaking. She wanted to see people. She wanted to hear footsteps on the sidewalk outside the boarding house. She wanted to talk, see smiles, and listen to the sound of people's voices. She wanted to study their clothes and learn their habits and listen to their stories. She was starved for people. She needed them.

Nell blossomed, moving quickly past her natural shyness, gaining a fragile poise. Her gray eyes brightened. Her step became quick and lively. Her face softened into a lovely picture of sad, peculiar strength mixed with hard gained wisdom. She laughed without rancor when the ladies asked her what brand of face powder gave her such a glow.

She studied her hair and worked with it, using a vinegar rinse to bring out the sheen and lighten the gray. She let it grow and wore it in new ways, in a coronet of braids, a French twist, and sometimes in a chignon at the nape of her neck.

She softened the look of her lanky frame by adding fuller collars and extra material to her plain, drab dresses. Margaret was delighted.

She suggested they make new dresses, and brought out buttery yellows, greens, and paisleys to choose from.

It wasn't long before the deep, shady porch of the boarding house became the favorite meeting place for the ladies of Cross Grove. Some of them donated their old rocking chairs to the large porch so they would all have a place to sit.

The porch shaded the ladies from the sun while they rocked and talked and watched the activities along Main Street in Cross Grove. Before long, the men congregated at the general store while the women assembled on the front porch of Nell's boarding house. Fall came, and Nell and the ladies sat on the boardinghouse porch watching colorful leaves drift to the ground.

Nell turned her back on Addition Jones the few times she saw him in town. He was nothing to her now. Each Sunday he sat like a large black boulder in the back pew of the church. He never talked to anyone when the service was over. He just walked out, got on his horse and rode away, same as the Smiths used to.

Chapter 10. Rocking Chairs

Back and Forth
Expansion

One winter afternoon, Nell stopped working on a dress and strolled to the front window. She pulled the curtain aside, contentedly watching the snow falling to the ground in lacy flakes. She imagined the soft plopping sound each snowflake made when it landed. Anyone who believed snow didn't have a sound, was never a child listening in the silence of an old red barn somewhere out on the edge of the world, waiting for something to change, for someone, anyone, to come visit.

Her heart and soul knew the sound of the first snow. The return of the white, come to cover all dark things with a white blessing that softened edges and eased pain and loneliness.

She remembered dancing in the snow by herself, not alone, at last; no one could dance in falling snow and feel alone, for she knew without a doubt that angels loved snow, too.

There's nothing like winter to bring peace to a body's soul, she thought, letting the curtain fall back across the window.

It was time to bathe and dress. Her new winter dress was made of green velvet with a sweetheart collar, large wrist cuffs, a fitted waist and a full skirt that brushed the tops of her new black shoes.

When she finished bathing, she dried off and assessed herself in the mirror. She'd washed her hair last night and brushed it shiny. She braided her hair and wove it into a neat crown around the top of her head, fastening it firmly in place. She looked this way and that in the mirror. The coronet lent a queenly, dignified air to her plainness. Her gray eyes look wider apart and her face more defined.

She slipped into undergarments and stockings, then slid the new dress over her head. She posed in front of the bedroom mirror. The green velvet deepened the color of her gray eyes. She studied her image. She knew she was plain and big. She knew she possessed good attributes, things such as a good character, but tonight she yearned to be within shouting distance of attractive.

She smiled at herself in the mirror and picked up the jar of expensive rose cream from Margaret. She unscrewed the lid and sniffed deeply. "Ah!" she sighed appreciatively. The sweet rose scent wafted through the air. She rubbed the heavenly smelling cream across the backs of her hands. It felt wonderful. She dipped more out and massaged it into her face and neck.

When she was ready, she strolled into the parlor to wait for Claude and Margaret. They were coming by to escort her to the Thanksgiving Dance at the Grange Hall.

She crossed to the window to watch the snow again. She lifted the curtain and looked out. Shocked, she jumped back and hid with a sinking heart. Addition Jones was stealing another rocking chair! She trembled with fear and rage. What he was doing didn't make any sense!

She chose to ignore him when he took the first two rocking chairs off the porch. She told herself he was taking them to replace the two rocking chairs she'd kept on the porch of the house she'd built on his property. He'd ordered her to bring them back when she told him what her father did to him. She never returned them, so he came and took them back himself. That made sense, so she let it go. But taking a third rocking chair didn't make any sense at all!

He took them right out in the open, as though he was doing nothing wrong. She watched from behind the curtain as he placed the third rocking chair in the back of his wagon, got in, and drove away without a glance towards the boarding house. She just bet he knew she was watching him.

A short time later, Margaret ran up the steps and in the house. She closed the door behind her and rubbed her hands together.

"Whoo! Claude's waiting for us. It's getting colder out there! Make sure you wear your warm coat!"

She stopped and stared at Nell.

"You're white as a ghost! What happened?"

"Nothing."

Nell turned away and went to the coat closet. No one knew about his theft of the rocking chairs. No one saw him carrying them away. Her heart pounded like a scared rabbit's when he took them. She should have stored the rocking chairs in the shed out back instead of leaving them on the porch after he took the first two. Now he had taken a third one! Something crazy and bad was going on underneath, and they were both a part of it. He was punishing her over her father, and she was letting him. She felt distant and helpless, wondering what he would do next.

A week later, Margaret was waiting in Nell's living room. They were due at a lady's guild meeting. Margaret heard steps on the porch, went to the window, and lifted the curtain. She watched in surprise as Addition Jones picked up a rocking chair and carried it off the porch. She felt Nell grab her arm with fingers of steel and pull her away from the window. Margaret jerked away from Nell.

"What's going on?"

"Don't go out there!" Nell commanded.

"What's Addition Jones doing here?"

Nell set her mouth in a grim line.

"He's taking another rocking chair."

"Why?"

"I don't know why!"

Margaret started for the front door. Nell grabbed her arm again.

"No! You can't! He's crazy!"

Margaret stopped and gave Nell a long look of indignant appraisal.

"How long has this been going on?" she asked sharply, hands planted on her hips.

"This is the fourth chair he's taken. I feel so ashamed! I can't stop him," Nell wailed. "I think he's doing this because I told him what my father did to him, and maybe he thinks I owe him."

Nell babbled on.

Margaret had noticed the pall Nell was under. She was losing weight and keeping secrets, and now Margaret knew why.

"So that's what's been going on! Well, it's got to stop!" she spoke sharply. "It's making you sick, Nell, don't you see?"

Nell lowered her head and didn't say anything. Margaret threw up her hands in exasperation.

Nell went to the window and lifted a corner of the curtain and looked out. She dropped the curtain back in place and grabbed her coat.

"He's gone! Let's just go to the meeting." She urged Margaret out the door and locked it behind them.

Early the next morning, Margaret opened the front door with her key. Carrying a rocking chair, she swept past Nell, marched into the empty back room by the kitchen, and set it down. One by one, she carried the rockers from the porch and stacked them in the little room. Then she closed the door.

"We'll put them in the shed later," she explained briskly to Nell. "There! Now that's over. Let's have some coffee and forget all about it!" Gratefully, Nell followed her into the kitchen.

But it wasn't over. A week later, Addition Jones drew to a stop in front of the boarding house. He sat on his wagon seat, studying the empty front porch like an ominous, forbidding black scarecrow. Nell watched him from behind the curtain. The game was over. Now he would drive away empty-handed and leave her alone.

She watched in shock as he climbed down from the wagon and ambled around the back of the boarding house, taking his time like the place was his, and he was doing absolutely nothing wrong.

"What? What is he doing?" she gasped to herself. Her mind reeled as she watched him walk back around the house carrying one of the heavy wood blocks that made up her back steps. He tossed it into the back of his wagon. Nell was completely dumbfounded. She listened to the thud of the wood block fall into the wagon. In her mind, she consoled herself.

It's only a step. A piece of wood. He'll leave now. What would he use someone else's wood step for?

But he didn't leave. He walked behind the house again. Rage broke past her frozen, mesmerized mind. Nell trembled with fury. *This insanity has got to stop! She would make it stop! No more!* She began to shake all over.

"My God, the man is insane!" she shouted.

Rage drove her through the house and out the back door where he was wresting another wood step from its place.

"You put that step down and get out of here and don't you ever come back!"

He ignored her shouted orders. He picked up the block of wood, hefted it to his shoulder, and started around the side of the house.

She ran back in the house, frantic with the need to hurt him, to stop him. She ran through the rooms looking for something to hurt him with. Her eyes lit on the small ironing board she used to press dress sleeves. It was slim and thick and made of heavy wood.

She ran through the front door and down the steps, the board held high in her hands. He was almost to his wagon. He turned and watched her run at him through the snow with the ironing board lifted high.

Quickly he tossed the block of wood into the back of his wagon and turned to face her. He waited for her with no expression at all. Suddenly he grinned. Nell thought he looked like an insane schoolboy who was just having some fun. She rushed at him and swung the ironing board at his head with all of her might.

He ducked, and she spun around in a full circle, hitting only empty air. She skidded to a stop in the snow and righted herself. He knocked the board out of her hands with a contemptuous flick of his wrist. Her heart pounded in her ears. She was determined to kill him any way she could.

She rushed him again, her hands clenched into fists. He stepped towards her, reached out and grabbed her fists. She found herself jerked up against his body. His arms around her were like steel vises. He groaned in her ear. She shoved herself away from the sick sound of it, and her feet slid out from under her. She fell in the snow and lay there, looking up at him.

From what seemed like a faraway distance, she heard Claude and Margaret's' angry voices. Dazed, she watched Claude step across her, grab Addition Jones and punch him in the face. He knocked him to the ground and sat on him, while Margaret helped Nell up. They fled to the safety of the boarding house porch and watched the two men.

Addition Jones lay like a sunken shadow in the snow. Nell saw how skinny he was, like a skeleton covered with dark skin. For a fleeting second, pity winged its dark, fluttering way through her being; she alone understood what he was and how he got that way. She understood his darkness and thinness, for she was carrying the same gauntness in her own soul. If she was cut open in that instant, a never-ending flood of tears would have started pouring out of her.

Addition Jones lay still, not fighting Claude, staring up at him with a mixture of sheer hatred and patience on his face. The same way she felt about him. His look washed her pity away and brought back her raging, fearful hate. She broke away from Margaret and skittered back and forth on the porch.

"Kill him, Claude!" she screamed before Margaret grabbed her and held her close. Claude ignored Nell's words.

"If you ever come near Nell again, I'll see to it you're put in jail or run out of this town! Shame on you for treating a woman like this! The people in this town have had enough of you! You stay out of my store and you better not go to church, either! You've got some bad mental problems, mister, and you better take them somewhere else! Go back to that fancy city. Maybe they'll put up with you acting crazy, but we won't put up with it here!"

Addition Jones lay in the snow, staring up at Claude, his face as blank and smooth as a slate. Claude let him up, and he stood and began leisurely brushing the snow off his clothes. Claude took a threatening step towards him. He stopped his insolent posturing, ran to his wagon, climbed up on the seat, and drove away.

Margaret and Claude pulled Nell into the living room.

"I've never seen anybody act like that," Claude shook his head.

Margaret voiced her opinion, "He's crazy! There's something bad wrong with that man! It goes beyond anything I've ever seen!"

Nell was filled with hopelessness. Her fear hadn't helped her. Her anger didn't change anything. Addition Jones was like an unnatural weather occurrence, like a tornado one could only handle by hiding in a storm shelter until it was over. Only he never ended or went away. She was living in fear of what he would do next. Now she realized he would never stop. She shuddered with helplessness and shame. She looked at Claude and Margaret sadly.

"I'll have to leave here. Maybe I can go someplace where he won't find me."

Margaret and Claude looked at each other.

"There must be something else we can do," Margaret stated firmly. But none of them came up with a solution.

Chapter 11. Rocks and Wood

Memorizing
Chastising

Addition Jones fled through the snow, his heart pounding with deep shame. *I am possessed!,* he shouted to himself. That was the only thing that could possibly explain his insane condition. In all of the years he'd spent refining and educating himself, accruing money, he'd always exercised the utmost discipline. He knew better than to do what he was doing to Nell. He berated himself all the way back to the farm, but in his heart and soul, the foul darkness stayed silent, waiting to spring again. Revenge or whatever darkness was awake in his soul would act again. It was an enemy he knew he could not conquer.

The next Sunday, he showed up for church and sat in his usual seat. Nell, Margaret, and Claude gave each other confounded looks and shook their heads.

"At least he's staying away from the boardinghouse. Maybe things will right themselves now," Nell said to Margaret in a tone of frail hope.

*

One night Nell was getting ready to for bed. She yawned and rubbed the tips of her fingers together. Too much sewing always made them feel flat and tingly. She glanced at the two long windows overlooking the little back yard behind the boardinghouse.

Under the sheer curtains that let in afternoon light were privacy shades. She pulled the shades, dimmed the kerosene lamp and changed into a flannel nightgown. She blew out the light and was climbing into bed when she noticed a movement out of the corner of her eye. She stopped and stared at the window.

"Maybe it's a wild animal of some kind," she murmured softly.

She tiptoed to the window and edged the privacy shade back an inch with her finger, and stared out into the darkness. The new snow made it easy to see the ground. She waited, not moving.

Just an animal trying to find shelter from the cold, she told herself, but her uneasiness persisted. A sixth sense held her to the window, watching and waiting. Finally, she saw a shadow moving. It poured itself like dark ink across the snow and slid slowly around the back of the house.

She watched, her heart pounding, eyes widening in horror as the outline of a man shaped itself against the back of the house. The outline crept toward the other window of her bedroom. She watched in terror as the shadow fell across the shade covering the window. She knew who it was. He was out there, leaning up against the window, his hand cupped to his face, trying to see into her bedroom.

Shocked, she watched him through the tiny crack in the shade. Her mind didn't know where to take his latest evil. He moved again, edging carefully towards the window she stood behind. She thought of his eyes making contact with hers and knew she would die if that happened. She eased the shade back into place and backed up slowly until she was sitting on the bed. She sat on the bed in the darkness and watched his shadow cross the second window and leave.

She waited a long time, frozen to the bed, before she was able to get up and lock the bedroom door. She lit the lamp, took the gun out of the closet, loaded it and propped it by the bed. Then she unlocked the door, slipped into the kitchen and found nails and a hammer. She nailed her bedroom windows shut and locked the bedroom door again. Exhausted from shock and fear, she blew out the lamp, crawled under the covers and fell asleep. A cold silence settled over the darkness.

Early the next morning, she nailed all the windows in the boarding house shut. She hammered small nails in places no one would notice. She searched in the shed out back until she found two-yard-long, thin pieces of wood and carried them into the kitchen. She peppered them full of long nails on one side and turned them over so the nails stood up. She carried them out back and placed each one on the ground, nails up, beneath the two bedroom windows. Then she made new curtains out of heavy, dark materials for all of the windows in the house and hung them up.

She locked her doors by dusk and was careful to take the gun out of the closet and prop it by her bed at night. She didn't go out back to find out if the boards did their job or not.

"My, your new curtains are nice!" Margaret said. "They'll keep the heat in this winter, but you'll want to take them down come spring because they're so heavy and make the house so dark. What made you think of it?"

Nell turned to the stove and picked up the coffee pot. She said, "Oh, I just needed a change."

When she finally went out back, she found the boards gone and the tracks of his boots in the snow beneath the bedroom windows. New snow came a few days later, and he didn't come back. Instead, he started coming into town to meet the train. He escorted the businessmen he met to the little restaurant directly across the street from Nell's boarding house. When their meetings were over, he left for the farm while the men he met retired to the only hotel in town for the night. They stayed strictly to themselves until the train carried them out of town the next morning. When he wasn't meeting someone at the train station, he was picking up packages and other items.

"Orders everything from Chicago," the porters and other workers at the station whispered to each other. "Too good to buy 'em here."

Nell knew he was keeping himself in front of her on purpose. He wanted her to think of him constantly and to live in terror of what he might do next. Though he never looked her way, he always stopped where she could see him. His grandstanding forced her to retreat to any place she couldn't see him, and he knew it.

She lost weight steadily from her tall, big-boned frame. The angles and planes in her face hollowed out. The sleepless nights she was enduring began to tell on her. Many days she couldn't concentrate at her old level, and Margaret was forced to pick up the slack in the sewing room. Her mind ran in never ending circles as her bright new world fell apart.

Where could she go? There was enough money, but there was no one, good or bad, to guide her now. She was snared helplessly in the closest, most personal relationship with him and couldn't stop it. She began to slowly disengage from everyone.

*

Claude and Margaret watched the innocent, untouched look in Nell's eyes change into a look of hurt awareness.

"What's wrong, Nell?" Margaret asked. "Tell me and let me help."

Nell shrugged and didn't answer. Margaret took her worries to Claude.

"We have to do something to help Nell before she gets worse! Have you noticed all the weight she's lost? She doesn't talk to me anymore. I just know it has something to do with Addition Jones!"

They came up with two plans. The first was for Claude to visit Addition Jones, try to talk to him and find out if he was still harassing Nell in some way.

Claude set out on his mission. He swung the buggy into the farmyard and drew to a stop. He looked around in dismay at the state the farm was in. The pretty little house was bare and forlorn. There were no curtains at any of the windows. Ragged weeds stood high around the house. The corral by the barn was empty. Claude shook his head in disapproval.

Addition Jones sure wasn't spending any money on the farm!

He started to climb out of the buggy, but suddenly a new thought crossed his mind. Mr. Jones might shoot him for trespassing. That was legal in this state. He felt a dark watchfulness surrounding him as he drove out of the yard, leaving the emptiness of it behind.

Later he told Margaret, "The man's crazy. Something's bad wrong out there. I knew it as soon as I drove in and saw the shape the place is in. That's why I left. It won't do any good to talk to him."

It was time for plan two. Time for Margaret to take over. She hounded Nell with questions while they sewed.

"What's going on? What is it you're not telling me? I thought you trusted me enough to let me help you."

She pursued her mission relentlessly until Nell finally broke down and cried out her secret.

*

Nell handed over the yellowed paper without protest. Margaret copied the address down and gave it back to her. Claude and Margaret set out early the next morning. They took a back road out of Cross Grove, carrying a letter of introduction from Nell. In it, she assured

Jason and Nola that Claude and Margaret Webster were her best friends; that the story they were bringing them was true.

*

Jason and Nola listened to the story of their son's behavior with mounting concern. They agreed with Claude and Margaret. He was acting dangerous and crazy. Jason's sternness softened and he spoke quietly, "It sounds like the intensity of the Traveler's blood he inherited from us is coming out in him. Passion, sensible or not, is part of Alexander's heritage."

He smiled at Nola, his dark eyes intense with love and admiration for her.

"We are a people of strong passions. When we have a big problem to solve, sometimes a sort of craziness sets in. We will find a way to help our son become sane again."

He spoke with confidence. A few days later, Jason, Nola, and Nell settled in at Claude and Margaret's house to spend the night. Jason and Nola left for their son's farm early the next morning. Nell, Margaret, and Claude went about their daily business as usual, knowing it would be a long day.

Jason and Nola stopped their buggy in the farmyard. The sun was shining. The morning air was welcoming, clear, and bright. They sat there waiting, but no one came out to greet them. Finally, they climbed out of the buggy and stood looking at the house. Just then, Addition Jones stepped out of the barn. They heard him and turned around just in time to watch him stumble to a dead stop.

*

He watched the old man take off his hat as though he was looking at something holy. Something began breaking up inside him as he stared at them. His deliberate meanness began ebbing away. He tried to stop it, but the meanness kept right on leaving. What the hell was he supposed to do without it? He relied on it through thick and thin. Anger, bitterness, and revenge insured his survival. They'd got him through every misery in life so far.

But the young boy who craved his true father would not be denied. The man he dreamed about stood in front of him again. The man who climbed the knoll above this farm, the man he ran from, the man who shouted "Son!" at him. The man he looked exactly like. That man stood beside a beautiful little woman the young boy in him could not bear to look at, or he would burst into tears and run into her arms.

For the first time in his lonely life, his soul was not alone. He knew it, and he was in hell trying to deny it. But his blood would not be denied. It rushed darkly through his veins, thrilled and magnetized at last by the right genetics standing in front of him. His blood sang out to the man and woman. Their Traveler's souls understood his. In that moment, he knew without a doubt they loved him deeply, and in their peculiar Traveler's way, they understood their bitter journeys alone as a way of God tempering him and them.

The odd knowing angered and confused him. In desperation, he dredged up an old piece of familiar bitterness. He would handle this the way people expected him to. These people would never know how deeply they affected him. Donning a mask of indifference meant his very survival many times, just like it did right now.

They will leave hating me like everyone else does! he thought. *That's good!* But his blood, bones, and heart broke at the possibility.

The tall, dark man in front of him interrupted his thoughts. He spoke in a mild voice, as though he was talking to a stranger about the weather.

"We're in town for a short visit with some friends. We thought you might like some company. It doesn't look like you get much out here."

The man looked around at the bleak and empty buildings. There was no livestock, no hay, nor any of the signs of more than a horse being kept on the place. No signs of a good, happy living.

"I thought it was time for you to meet us. My name is Jason Mennebar, and this is my wife Nola Songbird Mennebar. This is the second time you and I have met, but the first time for you to meet Nola."

He couldn't bear to look at the soft, dove-like woman clinging to the man's arm. He couldn't look into the dark eyes swimming with tears, eyes so much like his own. Instead, he stared down at the ground and scowled, resorting to the vernacular he learned from the Smiths as a child.

"Don't want no liars and thieves on my place," he growled.

The older man chuckled. Suddenly Addition Jones felt like a very young and foolish boy.

"You don't have any of that here, son. Just your own mother and father, your blood kin, standing right here in front of you."

His mind reeled at the words. He stared harder at the ground, clinging to it with his mind to keep from falling off the Earth. He didn't dare let himself look up or speak.

Nola took a step forward. She held a small frame in her hands.

"Son, I've got something to show you."

He threw out a hand to ward her off. She laid the framed picture on the ground and turned to Jason.

"I think it's time to take a turn around the yard, don't you?"

Jason nodded and took her arm. They began to stroll in a slow, dignified, very wide circle around him. Jason threw a sentence towards him now and then.

"We live two counties over, on a big farm. Everybody calls it the Mennebar place. The farm was passed down to us. It's been in our family for generations. Our ancestors were Travelers from the old countries in Europe. Your grandfather wanted us to pass the farm on to our children so it would stay in the family. But we only had one child, and that was you."

Jason's voice trailed off as Nola muffled a sob into his shirt sleeve.

Addition Jones stared down at the picture gripped tightly in his hands. He didn't remember picking it up.

"The man in the picture is your grandfather, Jem Mennebar," Jason said, giving a large, deliberate, theatrical sigh on purpose.

"He was a man burdened with too strong a feeling nature. When he worked himself up to feeling too intense about something, he had trouble controlling himself. Sometimes he didn't understand himself at all. The old genetic mysteries our people carry were strong in him. Sometimes he did things he knew was wrong at the time, things that didn't make sense to him or anybody else. But he always righted it in the end, after he figured out what was going on with himself. He was proud and strong-willed, and sometimes unforgiving."

Jason continued, "If anybody offended him, he took too long getting over it. But when he cared about somebody, he was charming, and it lasted for all time."

Jason knew he was talking too much, but it was a hell of a task to fit in what needed to be said. He watched out of the corner of his eye as anger, humiliation and wild emotions ran across his son's face. He sighed. He'd seen that intense display of feelings all too often on his own dear father's face.

"You're not doing anything that's giving anybody any cause to worry like your grandfather did, are you, son?"

He asked the touchy question and watched his son bend over like an old man and lay the picture back down on the ground. His son straightened and gave them a bleak look. Then he turned his back on them, walked towards the barn but detoured to a bale of hay by the corral. He sat down on it, leaned against a rail, and turned his head away.

They watched him with breaking hearts. They wanted to draw closer to their boy, but they didn't dare try. He didn't look too big, or old, or rawboned, or skinny, or mean, or ugly, to them. He was their precious son! They were there to protect him, to explain his own odd, passionate nature to him, to stop him from his madness, to help him understand it. He looked so fragile, like a person who might fracture if one more thing was put on him.

Nobody knew what to do next. The losses each one of them had suffered because of his kidnapping turned and ticked painfully through the silent air, shared at last with each other in kinship. Long and slow, but inevitable, a healing began between a mother, father, and their child. No greater love could have begun it. It was a good start.

A long time passed. At last Jason stirred. It was time to go forward from what was once lost. He draped an arm protectively around Nola's shoulders. He knew it was too soon to speak to his son like a stern, loving father calling his beloved son to task, but it had to be done. Ruefully, he spoke in a stern voice, one a father used to his son when his son was doing something wrong.

"The men in our families have always been honorable. You are one of them, even though you weren't raised by us and taught how to be in the world. If you want something, you must be honest about it to yourself, or you will never get it. If you can't have it, then let it go in peace. It is not your right to take what is not willing to be yours, nor is it your right to be less than who you are."

Having begun, Jason was bound to continue. He told his son, "You've been mixed up about a lot of things for a long time, with every just cause a man could ever have. Now it is time for you to become who you always have been. It's time to stop what you are doing to yourself and her, and we will help you all we can."

His son's head jerked up. He glared at them. They knew what he was doing to Nell? His mind worked rapidly. She'd told on him. That's the only way they could have known. Anger and humiliation brought him to his feet.

"Git' off a' my property!" he ordered, through gritted teeth. "And don't ever come back!"

Nola sighed. They never got the chance to tell him his real name. She walked past the picture of Jem Mennebar laying on the ground but didn't pick it up.

Chapter 12. Counting Shadows

Seen
Square Pegs

He paced the yard furiously after they left. So, they came to call him off Nell, did they? Like a damned cur dog! That was the only reason they showed up! For somebody else, not him! They waited until he was doing something wrong before they bothered to come and see him!

"Their son!" he sneered to himself. He noticed the picture on the ground. He'd forgotten it. He stared at it. It was full of a quiet, steady darkness alien to him. It held a new truth, offered him a new understanding, a new beginning, but he already was who he was!

So they wanted to replace him with a nice, good, gently raised, passive son. That's what they wanted to get back after all these years. Well, wouldn't that be just dandy for them! Then they wouldn't have to face up to what he'd gone through while he was growing up without them!

Memories of the cold and the heat and the never-ending work he suffered through to get to where he was now, flooded his mind. He'd paid his dues and a hell of a lot more! His fury mounted. The small boy inside of him, his voice shaky and dim and in need of love, protested, but he ignored his pleas.

His body trembled and jerked. He had to do something, anything! He bent and clawed up a clod of dirt and threw it at the barn wall. The dirt bounced and shattered. He raced across the yard and into the fields. His feet carried him over the land and along the fence rows. He jumped fences, jerked things up out of the ground and threw them. He cursed the Smiths. He cursed everybody he could think of, especially Nell and Grady Miller.

His rage spent, he stopped and looked around. He was standing on the knoll above the house. He barked out a short laugh. Here was where it all started. He had come full circle, in spite of himself. Damn the Fates!

He stared down at the bare, prim little house below, remembering how it felt when he first moved in. The scent of hope and cleanliness lingered everywhere. Some of it was still there, tranquil and pretty, in spite of the neglect he dealt the house. The way she designed and built the house suited him, and oh, how he fought liking it! But it was cozy, clean, and convenient. The windows were in the right places. She'd framed the best views of the farm, using the windows to make it look like a private, rustic country paradise. The large, generous pantry, the sensible, comfortable, well-equipped kitchen, the large yet somehow cozy living room, all of it suited him.

His thoughts shifted. Well, he could be sure Nell hated him after all he did to her! He tromped down the hill to the house, stomped out of his boots, hung up his coat, and crossed to his large chair. He slammed his vexed body down into his chair and stared at the empty fireplace while old, bitter memories flooded his mind.

*

The old Smith folks were forever sour and dry. They never told him one word about their past. He never knew their people's names or where they came from. All that existed in his world was them, and they'd kept him like a dog, handing him food through the screen door, never letting him come in the house after he was old enough to be kenneled in the barn.

He remembered the few sounds in the Smith's grim, silent house. The clock ticking on the mantel, the scrape of chairs, the sound of dishes and housework being done.

There was never any music in his life, humming or singing or conversation. No touching, no gentle sighs, no words of kindness, no love. Just the infernal silence, stretching out long and tense, day after day.

Without knowing what it was he was feeling, he was relieved when he was permanently banished to the barn. He was desperate to get away from the dead, stiff silence the Smiths lived in. He must have been seven when it happened, maybe eight. He didn't know his age or when he was born. There were never any birthday celebrations for him-or them.

After he moved to the barn, at last there were sounds and warm bodies and companions. The cows made soft, soothing sounds. The horses moved and stomped and blew out their breath. The hay crinkled, the straw squeaked. The birds sang, and the cows bawled or whuffed in contentment when they ate. He slept on the hay in the cow stalls or up in the barn loft in a corner, content to listen and learn from the sounds made by Nature and the animals on the farm.

Like a father would, the wind blew and made him cool down when he became too desperate. The sun warmed his lanky frame into soothing moments of smoothed out muscles, the moon smiled down on him with the relaxed demeanor a mother gives her child to nourish him.

The snow covered his miseries with white, making it inconsequential that he was alone.

He washed in rain water in summer. In winter, he skated across the skinny little frozen creek wandering across an edge of the farm property, wearing worn out boots and a ragged coat. He leaned into the warm sides of the cows when he milked them. Their comforting touch made him sigh with relief. He groomed the horses and scratched the pigs' backs and smoothed the chickens' feathers to see what they felt like. He held downy chicks and felt the tender, sharp bite of their tiny feet clutching onto to him, as though they needed him too. He searched out the wild animals on the farm and learned their habits. Some he was able to touch, some not. The sounds, warmth, the touching and the seasons combined, kept him surviving.

But after a while, his desperate longing for human companionship became overwhelming. It drove him back to the house, and he began sneaking into it as soon as the old folks left for church on Sunday morning. He was nine or so the first time he sneaked into their house. He simply joggled the front door and found it opened, despite their locking it before they left.

Fearing they would discover something missing or out of place, he never touched their food or anything else, though he wanted to badly. If they found out he was in their house while they were gone, they would find a way to lock him out permanently.

Every Sunday, the theft of their space became his church time. Their house became his church. The Smiths had given him a worn-out Bible. Mrs. Smith taught him to read and write well enough to understand some of it. Their sole purpose was to make him behave, using the Good Book to do it.

Every Sunday morning, except when winter snow blanketed the porch and the Smiths would have seen his footprints, he sneaked into their house. He listened to the ticking of the large clock on the mantel above their fireplace. He looked through the rooms. In time, he learned the texture and feel of everything in the house. He touched the handles of skillets and pots and pans; he ran his fingers over the smooth, cold insides of them, craving food and warmth, smells and nurturing. The old woman must have touched them a thousand times in her life.

Mrs. Smith. Mr. Smith. That's what they made him call them. He didn't know their first names until the funeral. Hester and Abraham. He felt of the old man's heavy flannel shirts. They carried the musty smell of him. Once he tried on a shirt and wished he could take it back to the barn and keep it.

They always called each other "Woman" and "Man." They rarely spoke to each other or him; they spoke only as needed to instruct him. He was a boy whose very existence depended on following the stinginess of their dry, emotionless instructions.

His search deepened, and over time, there wasn't anything in the house he didn't know about. He kept on with his treasure hunt, but he never found the prize. After he searched through bureau drawers and all of their papers and everywhere else for a clue as to who he was, he finally gave up.

The search for who he was became a meaningless ritual. His name and history were nowhere in their house. His clothes and his few personal belongings were not a part of their lives, except as a servant who lived out in their barn. He did not exist as a human being to them. He did not exist to God. The house ceased to be a church, a place where God might take him in and finally tell him who he was. He stopped sneaking into the house on Sundays and began spending his time in his little back room or out in the fields.

But he needed more; the emptiness still rattled inside him. At first, he tried whittling animals out of wood. He was fair at it, but it was too limiting for him. A natural artist, he noticed the colors of things. He carried clay from the creek and painted the walls of his little room with it, but it wasn't colorful enough. He searched and found slate rocks and scraped out pictures of birds and trees with them on the walls of his room.

Over time, he quit wondering about much of anything and accepted his Fate. He cut himself off from the rest of humanity, who didn't want him, and stored his natural passion and intensity in a place only he could reach.

He turned for comfort once more to the birds and horses and cows and the other animals living on the farm. The wind blew, the snow fell. Storms crossed the fields leaving shadows, but the sunlight always returned. The animals clucked and groaned and bawled. They all lived their lives together, and he survived.

Chapter 13. Paul's Promise

Crossroads
Value systems

His young years fled by without any change until the Sunday morning Paul slid into the yard on his skis. He recalled the sweetness of the cookies and the sound of the harmonica Paul carried in his pocket that first visit. Sugar and sound were powerful things!

Paul was young and happy, big and hearty. He'd carried laughter and good humor into the yard with him. Paul saw life as a place to have a good time, no matter what it brought you. Paul taught him to read better and to think again.

Paul gave him the bird books. What a gift they were! The books opened his heart to the color and beauty he longed for. He was awed by the deep, bright colors and the grand richness of the pictures. His Bible held no pictures. It was filled with black and white words holding no meaning for him except punishment.

"The Bible is the only book allowed in the Smith's house," he said to Paul when he gave him the bird books to keep.

Paul laughed. "Guess you'll have to keep 'em hid. Why, there are lots of picture books in this old world even better than these bird books!"

His heart flowered with Paul's words. Elated, he began to share his own world with Paul. He showed him the bird nests in the fence rows and secret places on the farm no one else knew about. They spent two precious hours together each Sunday when the old folks were gone to church.

They were both young, and the blood ran hot in their veins as they jumped fences and laughed in his little back room. Paul taught him many things. Paul was his best friend, his only friend. Paul's attention to him and his laughter and affection stirred him back into wanting to be with people.

*

But in what seemed like only the blink of an eye, Paul started talking about a girl he knew. He quit coming out to the farm. He remembered being bewildered and terribly hurt. He was desperate to keep his friendship with Paul. He tried everything he could think of. He went into town with Paul, and later, he slipped into a back pew of the church and waited for Paul to notice him. He wore his best clothes, a pair of brown pants too short for him, a worn gray work shirt, and barn boots.

Paul was surprised to see him in church but friendly. The old folks acted like they didn't see him; they ignored him, got in their buggy and headed home after church.

Paul invited him for Sunday dinner in a few weeks. The delicious food and talk and warmth and laughter surrounding him felt like a miracle. The pastor gave him a new Bible and the barber cut his hair. He returned to the farm later and later on Sunday afternoons.

He was being with people, but he wanted Paul back. He wanted just the two of them and nobody else, like it used to be. Months passed while he waited. Finally, he realized Paul wasn't coming back. Paul was in love with the girl he sat with every Sunday. She was all he cared about.

In his youthful desperation, he made a shortsighted plan. He would have either Paul or the girl, and when Paul was alone, they would be friends again, like they used to be. He tried for Paul's girl and lost.

He remembered the day the old man tried to take the buggy whip to him in front of everybody at church. The old man ordered him never to go to church again, to keep to his place on their farm. The whole congregation stood outside, watching. Nobody tried to stop it, he thought bitterly, as was usual with the fine, upstanding folk of Cross Grove. Bitterly, he'd grabbed the whip away from the old man and broke it in two.

Then the house burned down with the Smiths in it. He was working in the back fields when it happened. Smoldering cinders and a charred black wood shell were the only things left on the foundation where the house stood by the time he got there. The town believed he started the fire. They turned their backs on him and treated him like a murderer.

Their hate finally forced him off the farm. He left the farm and Cross Grove behind and rode away into the unknown, a skinny, scared scarecrow of a kid who'd never been out in the world, starting out on his own.

He recalled the deep shock that ran through him when Nell told him what her father did to him and the Smiths.

Grady Miller, foul kidnapper and murderer! It was a good thing Grady Miller was dead, or he would have hunted him down like the damned animal he was and slit his throat and dumped him in the woods to be torn apart by wild animals!

His eyes roamed around the living room. He deliberately let the farm run down to get rid of the good things Nell did to it. But everywhere he turned, he saw signs of the hope she'd seeded into it. Hope meant for herself, or for him? She said she'd built the house for him. It was a question he asked himself every day. The hope she planted stayed in his face; it followed him wherever he went.

No matter that the cow and pigs were gone, there were hollyhocks blooming beside their empty pens. Wildflowers and rosebushes nipped along the porch edges in fragrant, hopeful abandon. No matter that the inside of the house was empty except for his few necessities, the sunlight still spilled warmly across polished wood floors and fluted across white walls in carefree bands.

The fireplace mantel was solid and tight and simple. When he looked at it, he never saw or heard the ornate, ticking clock the Smith's kept on their mantel. A clothesline was strung through new fruit trees growing up to shade the back of the house. The doors swung open to the left instead of the right. The smells of spices, milk and vinegar permeated the walls of the pantry.

He didn't understand why he stayed or why he did the things he was doing. He was never interested in courting any woman. That part of his self was one he never expected to experience. He didn't believe in that kind of love. So when did he start believing Nell belonged to him? He turned away from that thought and back to his memories.

After he fled the farm in his youth, every job he took turned to gold for him. The women turned to him too. But he never wanted any of them past a physical need on a weary night.

He used money to learn to speak properly, to dress expensively and conservatively. He hired tutors and willingly underwent being properly educated in books and matters of the world. He learned about money, his solicitors were top notch. Rarely did he let himself acknowledge the bitter, bereft young boy in him, still waiting to be loved.

When memories of the farm overcame him, he changed his conservative, expensive clothes for those of his childhood. He stayed away from people he knew and held the new bird books he'd bought in memory of the books he'd hid beneath the boards in his little room the day he fled the farm.

Hell, he didn't know why he took the damn rocking chairs! He shook his head at himself. At the time, he told himself they were part of something stolen from him, something that was his. But he didn't stop at two; he needed to take more, but more than two didn't make any sense! Then Nell took the chairs off the porch, so he stole her back doorsteps while she watched. He groaned. To make it worse, in the deepness of a winter night, he prowled around the back of her house!

He shook his head in horror at himself. He went back to her house twice more before he was able to stop his nocturnal stalking. She knew he'd been there and set out nail boards and put up curtains he couldn't see through. His mind turned to Jason Mennebar. Jason scolded him like a father scolds a son, and he liked it.

He looked around and sighed. His own food and sheltering warmth, such as it was, lay here in Nell's little house. He couldn't risk any more craziness with her. It was time for him to leave this farm and never look back. Empty words, because he knew he couldn't do it. He couldn't leave because of Nell. She'd changed his farm into what it should have been when he was a child.

She'd retrieved and revived his old dreams for him without ever meeting him or knowing if he was still alive or worth it. He mattered to her, and he'd responded to her hope with meanness and cruelty. Yes, she once cared. But not anymore.

*

Nell dragged the bedding outside to air out in the spring sunshine. Snow white sheets draped her clotheslines. New curtains covered her bedroom windows. The walls were freshly papered with the pink rose wallpaper pattern her mother liked. Her mother's quilts were stacked neatly on new white painted shelves between the two bedroom windows.

191

She didn't see Addition Jones all winter, not since the Mennebars visit. She hoped she never saw him again. She didn't feel guilty over what her father did to him anymore. The fact was, she too, was a victim of her father's relentless, never-ending evil.

Addition Jones disgusted and repelled her. She didn't care why he did things. Craziness couldn't be cured, just avoided. It was over, and she was glad. If he ever bothered her again, she wouldn't keep it a secret. She would turn him over to the sheriff. That part was settled. But another part wasn't.

She avoided thinking about him because every time she did, a little voice kept slipping past her righteousness, insisting there was something to thank him for. She hated thinking about it for she knew it took root the instant he'd grabbed her tight against him and groaned. No man had ever held her that close, in rage or in love.

She fought it, but the new awareness grew, whispering its way along the edges of her consciousness in a careful, perilous journey of survival. It was the reason she wallpapered her bedroom and laid out her mother's quilts. She felt the trailing touches of it when she smoothed the soft fabric of a new dress over her hips. It was the reason she studied herself in the mirror; the reason she arranged her hair in new ways to compliment her clothing.

She felt it when Margaret measured her for a dress and when she was measuring customers. She'd inadvertently given and received more touch since they started their business than she'd ever gotten in her life.

The soothing sounds of healthy women's voices, talking and laughing, instead of her mother's whining and hot, ailing touch, closed the tainted emotional distance she'd lived in. The brief, tender, impersonal touches of their kind hands steadily smoothed away the years of rough stone formed around her needy heart.

Her body changed along with her heart, a little at a time, though she fought it. Latent hormones flowed. Sometimes, when she was adjusting a collar or hem, like an adolescent, she wondered how it was for the woman in front of her to be in the bed with her man at night; the speculation made her blush. She wondered if the woman's soft, soothing voice tamed him. Sometimes, she thought of herself slipping between cool sheets where the warmth of a man lay waiting for her.

But she was old in this world of women who married young, she told herself. That time was past for her. She was a spinster, wasting her years on her father, then on Addition Jones. Now all that was left was this life.

*

Nell looked around the Grange Hall, enjoying the sounds of music and laughter at the annual Spring Dance. The night flew by until she felt a sudden shift in the energy. Something was wrong. She looked around the hall and saw Addition Jones lounging in a dim corner. He was leaning against a post, watching her. Her eyes darkened into a gray storm. Dressed in new clothes that fit him, she could have sworn they were dark gray instead of dead black. His hair was freshly cut. She wondered what kind of trouble he would start. Anger ran through her like a sharp, heated knife. She felt a hand touch her arm. Claude swept her into the circle of people on the dance floor.

He watched her all evening. Claude and Margaret escorted her to the boarding house. They went in with her to make sure she was safe. After they left, she locked the door, changed into her night clothes, climbed into bed, and promptly went to sleep. There was a gun by her bed, and she didn't give a damn anymore.

Chapter 14. Breaking Away

Alchemy
Rust

Addition Jones was breaking rocks in the south pasture. The thin layer of soil in the pasture covered piles of gray shale. Skinny, tough grass grew between the piles of shale. He told himself he was improving it.

Each morning at sunrise, he crossed the fields to the small south pasture; each day he carried different kinds of hammers and spent his day pounding the gray shale into smithereens, releasing the pink insides to the sun. He worked furiously until the sun was almost straight above him. Then he quit and went to the barn to do the few chores that needed doing every day.

When the chores were done, he went to the house and ate, didn't matter what it was. Whatever was the easiest and handiest. Then back to the south pasture and breaking up the tender, brittle, thin gray rocks with their delicate pink and gold insides. At the end of each day, he stood amid shining, shattered pieces of pink and gray rock, looking at them. Why was he doing this? Weary to the bone, he went back to the house each evening, washed up, ate, and fell into an exhausted sleep.

His black mood never let up. He felt sorry for himself; he knew he'd earned that right. He'd lived through and seen enough to break any man, and he didn't want any more of it.

Even after all he'd been through, nobody gave a damn! God didn't give a damn. Never did. Well, he was who he was, and that was all there was to it!

The gray shale rocks broke, the chips flew. He hated everyone and everything. Bleak thoughts dogged him while he worked. He should have stayed away from town. He shouldn't have gone to the dance. He rode to Benton and got a haircut. He wore a new gray suit the color of the doves he'd watched from his office window in Chicago. Doing those things, so simple in themselves, just made it worse. No wonder they thought he was dangerous. He was!

Dreams filled with rage and longing stalked his nights. He dreamed the little house was his only sanctuary. He dreamed of his mother's yearning face looking back at him from the buggy as she and Jason drove away. She was shouting something back at him. Was it his real name?

He was a man who knew how mean worked. He'd grown up under the iron fists of two of the meanest thieves and misers who ever lived.

They'd stolen his birthright and hoarded almost all he needed to survive from him. They'd almost killed him off, while the damned town looked the other way and let them.

He'd suffered a lifetime of pain. For years he was barely touched, only by unloving hands when necessary. Those who kept him barely spoke to him. He never knew of an affectionate word to pass the Smiths' mouths. No gestures, no good words for each other or him.

After weeks of backbreaking work in the south pasture, he was no better. He realized something had to give or he would die, and he was close to not caring which way it went. He fled back to the little house, his only solace, and climbed the porch steps.

Exhausted almost beyond living, he sat down at the kitchen table and laid his head down on his arms. It was time to give up. He wondered how to go about not existing. He didn't trust God, but if there was a force of some kind running this world, he needed a miracle to get out of the place he was stuck in. Dead or alive, it was time to move on.

He gave up and moved into the inevitable unknown. He waited for it to take him away. He assumed he would stop breathing. Instead, he felt himself relaxing and breathing deeply, thoroughly. He felt distant and sleepy, as though nothing was important. It was okay if he just rested. This house belonged to him. It was his home. He felt protected. He relaxed into the house. He gave in and let his life force go where it would.

He felt a gentle touch on his arm. Someone gracious and filled with love stood near him. He'd heard of angels, but never felt one's presence before. He couldn't move his head to look. He guessed he wasn't supposed to. He felt the heat emanating from their touch. Something warm and soothing traveled down into the blood and bones of his arm. Relaxing, wonderful energy spread upwards, leaving heat and color in its wake. He felt the different parts of himself start to hum in response.

His exhausted body grabbed at it, though he couldn't move. The warmth traveled into his chest and settled around his heart. A sort of melting began. He opened his eyes and looked in astonished awe at the light surrounding him. It was full of translucent figures of angels and children laughing and dancing around him, holding small pink shards of shale in their hands. They touched him with the pink and gold remnants, pouring heat and color and warmth into him. He watched them with gratitude and wondered if they were lost children with broken hearts, like him.

His heart opened and he cried, knowing that yes, once they were like him. He accepted them in. At last, no matter what happened to him, from this minute onward, he would never be alone again. They would be with him. He closed his eyes and sobbed. When he finished, he looked around again. The children and angels were gone. He was exhausted and filled with gratitude. He got up, staggered off to his bed and fell into a deep sleep.

He slept off and on for two days before he was fully awake. He was ravenous. He went to the kitchen and cooked himself a huge meal. He noticed his movements were smooth and deliberate again, not jerky and tight like before.

While he cooked and ate, he puzzled over his dreams. He dreamed about birds while he slept. The dreams came in an orderly sequence, one after the other, with a single-minded purpose.

In the first dream, he was holding the three bird books Paul gave him. He turned the pages over and over again, admiring the bird drawings.

In the second dream, he was sitting in his little room out in the barn, holding the bird books against his chest. He was suffering terrible anguish caused by his years of deprivation. For solace, he opened the bird books one by one, turning the pages. The birds in each picture came alive and flew out of the picture. Each one selected the piece of hurt it was meant to destroy; grabbed it, ripped it out of him and into shreds, then flew away with the ragged remnants.

In his third dream, the ceiling of his little room expanded out into a blue sky. The walls darkened into indigos and reds, with trees and foliage growing beyond them. The birds from the books lit on branches and spread their beautiful plumage out for him to admire. The birds paraded and sang, and the trees and leaves branched out. The trees and leaves changed colors and shapes. More birds circled them and lit. The colors and shapes of the birds awed him. He reached out to touch them. Paint poured from his fingertips, coloring the birds even brighter. Then the birds were flying, circling the inside of his little room again. He looked around. The walls and ceiling and door were covered with paintings of the birds and *he* had painted them!

He understood clearly that he painted them to keep himself sane; to keep himself from doing bad things to Nell or anyone else.

In his fourth and final dream, he stood in his little room, staring at his bird paintings as the acceptance seeped into him that Goodness was Beauty. He allowed himself to touch, to feel intensely - just for an instant - his own Goodness. He *was* a good man, and someday, somehow, his Goodness would help the lost children who came to him in the house and saved him from dying. Suddenly he was filled with purpose. He knew if he wanted to keep feeling powerful and Good, he would have to paint the birds.

What? He shouted to himself in his dream. *Don't be ridiculous!* He laughed at the ludicrous idea of himself with a palette in hand, posturing in front of a canvas. If the boardrooms he ruled in Chicago could see what he was dreaming, they'd laugh him out of town! He dismissed the idea. It was the most ridiculous thing he'd ever heard. He liked power and money, and he already possessed plenty of both! Painting birds was one of the most powerless things he could think of doing!

Suddenly the children were dancing around him again, touching him, melting his rigid, proud thinking. He remembered his lonely childhood and the birds and animals that kept him alive.

It was not his Fate to know anything else. He was to honor Nature's wish. His heart suddenly understood the wisdom Nature was asking of him, and he found himself painting the birds, feeling purposeful and in control of his heart and life, for he was helping the dancing children like he was never helped. They needed him.

He finished eating and rushed off to town to buy the basics so he could get started. When the children playing in the streets cawed at him, he acknowledged them grimly. He accepted his place in their life. He was an old black scarecrow-one with hidden talents!

He hurried home, eager to begin the new work ahead of him. But he couldn't get started. He put the brushes and paints down. For some reason, it wasn't time yet. He wandered the farm aimlessly, trying to figure out what he needed to do before he could pick up a brush and begin learning to paint.

That night, before he went to sleep, he asked the children what to do. They sent him a dream about a Monster and the completion that needed to take place. He was to let his instincts guide him. The next morning found him riding Midnight with his camping gear tied behind him.

He rode to the small town of Prairie Creek near Nell's farm. He bought a large sack of their purest salt and a few other things at the general store and asked for directions to the local cemetery.

Wildflowers and weeds bloomed higher than the tops of the gravestones in the small, neglected cemetery. He waded through the heavy, hot air, his long black boots parting the tall weeds.

He searched until he found the thin, cheap headstone. It was already crumbling. He knelt down and grimly studied the name on the plain, ugly stone. Grady Miller. His worst enemy. The man who stole his birthright from him. Why, he didn't even know his birthday! Oh, how he hated him! He let the hate rise in him before he jerked off his boots and stomped on the grave to let the hate run down through him and into the grave beneath his feet. He stomped until the poisonous hate emptied itself into the grave of his enemy, sent back where it belonged. No longer would he carry hatred that hurt himself and everybody else around him for this Monster! It ended here and now!

When he was done, he put his boots back on and ripped the wildflowers and grass away from the cheap gray stone and the rest of the grave until it lay completely bare.

Wherever Grady Miller was now, whatever hell he lived in, it was his alone to bear now, not Nell or his anymore. They'd suffered enough. That suffering ended here, today!

It was time to do a righteous thing. He stood up, stepped back and studied the grave. The gray headstone stood cheap and thin and ugly in the hot sun. The grave was bare, with nothing growing on it. That was good. Now it was time to make sure no flowers or blanket of grass would ever grow again over the evil man moldering beneath that bare dirt. He opened the large bag of pure salt and sprinkled every grain of it carefully over the headstone and the bare, ugly grave while he repeated what he remembered of The Lord's Prayer over and over.

When he was done, he stood back. Nothing grew in salted ground. Anyone seeing this grave would read the name, see its bareness, and know a ritual had been performed over it because something evil lay there. That was good.

His eyes swept over the little cemetery. It looked like no one ever visited here anyway. He knew Nell never would. She'd probably put the gravestone over him to keep track of where he was. From now on, Grady Miller would be alone much longer than he'd forced them to be. That was good.

He turned on his heel and left to start his next errand. There were more things to finish. He rode into the yard of the farm where Nell grew up and looked around. A tall, lanky man and a busy looking little woman came out of the house. She was drying her hands on a kitchen towel.

"You got any chickens for sale?" he inquired, showing a handful of money because he was a stranger and most people didn't like the way he looked. "I'm a bachelor, and I need a few hens and a rooster to get started." They nodded eagerly. He asked to look around the farm.

"I knew the people that used to live here, and I'll be glad to pay you for your time."

They showed him the house and garden and barn and tried to sell him a few more things to go with the chickens. He studied everything closely. All of it was clean, snug, secure and well-planned. He saw the fine hand and intelligence of Nell all over the little farm.

There was no feeling or sign on the farm of the evil Grady Miller once carried. It was gone, and he suspected Nell somehow erased it. So, she had taken care of that part already. He didn't have to do it. For a fleeting instant, he let himself admire her.

He rode away with a brace of squawking chickens slung across the saddle in front of him. He turned them loose as soon as he was out of sight of the house.

*

A few days later found him hiding on another knoll, watching another farmhouse below. He watched the woman hanging up clothes and the man strolling across the yard to help her. He yearned to hear snatches of their conversation, but they were too far away.

When the sound of their laughter reached him, he looked away, a bitter grimace on his turned down mouth. He camped out, rode to the knoll, hid and watched the man and woman going about their daily lives. There were long, silent days when the only thing he watched was the empty yard. He wondered where they went and what they were doing. One day, it was over. Whatever was holding him there was gone. He broke camp and rode back to his farm.

A day later, he headed for the barn and his little room. It was time to take the lock off the door and see if the bird books were still under the floorboards. He unlocked the door and pulled it open, stepped inside and looked around. Everything was covered with dust. He braced himself against the flood of memories crowding him, waiting to be felt and fed again.

He pushed them away, pulled up the floorboard and lifted out his beloved bird books. He left quickly, locking the door behind him. He carried the bird books back to the house and placed them carefully on the table by his chair. He touched them gently. They belonged here, in this house, for they were the foundation, unknowingly laid long ago, of the change he needed to make today.

He made long lists, sealed them in envelopes, rode to town and mailed them. Then he went home, studied the bird books, walked the land, and waited. The packages started coming in on the train. They came wrapped in brown paper with no return address, just as he instructed.

He was a spare and meticulous man. He did not like dirt or disorder. Although he liked luxury, he didn't like it to be fussy. He unwrapped and broke open boxes. He unpacked and sorted. He carried and placed everything where he wanted it, in the house and out in the barn.

The painting books came in last. There were dozens of them, thick with instructions, wisdom, beautiful pictures and sometimes, huge egos. He laughed out loud as he introduced them to their three elders, the three bird books stacked on the table beside his chair before he added them to the books layered in the bookcase by the fireplace.

He built a table in the barn, placing it where the light was best for painting. Finally, he began. At the first stroke of his brush, he felt a vast sense of relief. He painted and read and learned.

He couldn't get the paint on fast enough. He was always running out of supplies. He needed more brushes, more mediums and more paint thinner. He rode farther and farther away to get what he could find and ordered the rest, for he suspected the people of Cross Grove would wonder if he was setting fires again if he bought paint thinner in town.

At night he dreamed of the birds, and they slowly healed something wounded in him. He rode with the beautiful birds as they flew and soared into bright futures he never imagined possible, and into ancient pasts filled with wonder. Sometimes they were so beautiful he woke up gasping. In time, he realized they were teaching him about the power of true spiritual beauty and how it both healed and divided.

Tentatively, he began to trust in a Divine Force. He couldn't have his parents or Nell, but he could have the birds. They wouldn't hurt him. And, he told himself, he could throw the paints away any time he wanted to. He could paint over the little back room and the canvases tacked up on the walls. Nobody would ever know, for didn't he have a reputation for being the ugliest, most evil man Cross Grove ever knew?

Why, there was no beauty to him! He was just a murderer, a Beast! He had a reputation to maintain! His emotional pain left him when he picked up a brush. The beautiful birds didn't visit his dreams when he didn't paint. The message was clear.

He scraped and brushed and cursed, all the while holding the solitary, desolate Beast he believed himself to be at bay, at least while he was painting. When he painted, he was just a man instead of a Beast, a painter filling his lonely, isolated life with lovely riches money couldn't buy! Intense blues, glossy blacks, dark greens, and deep purples offset with red and yellows filled the canvas covered walls of his little barn room in raw, crude, compelling colors.

He was impatient, constantly cursing his clumsiness and lack of knowledge. But he kept working at it, and because of it, ugly pieces of his old, barren life began breaking free.

One day, while he was working on a painting, an old, miserable piece of him broke free. He felt it float up in the air like a balloon, then leave. He didn't know, nor need to know, what it was. He had processed enough pain to last a lifetime, and any ugliness wanting to leave without causing him misery was free to go!

He barked out a short laugh. He stopped painting and grinned at himself. He'd never thought of himself as having a sense of humor. He laughed again in unholy glee at what he was hiding from other people. If only they knew! He laughed with relief at how his pain stopped when he painted. Such a silly thing to cure the pain of a lifetime!

Sometimes for just an instant, figures of happy children danced across the edge of his vision. He grinned at the irony of a personality like his doing something like painting and seeing children who didn't run away from him. But the sparks of laughter always died too soon, and the loneliness returned.

He knew people thought he was violent. He knew people saw him as large and ugly, and they believed it was okay for him to be kept in isolation and cursed with foul looks from them.

What if he'd discovered painting before the old folks burned up in the fire, and he didn't become older than sin from loving them, no matter what they did to him? They wouldn't have let him keep at it. The Beast painting Beauty. Hah! He chuckled thinly at the thought, hollow as a waiting pond reed, swaying in his black farm boots, tapping them on the barn floor, sometimes crying or cursing, but still painting.

His thick black hair grew long and matted, and he stopped bathing. He liked the sour smell of his own sweat. Sometimes he stalked out of the barn and threw himself, clothes and all, into the water trough by the corral. He told himself he just wanted to be clean. But he knew he was starting to play again, like he'd played out in Nature as a child. He couldn't curb that rampant child Nature had raised and was still blessing.

When he wasn't painting, he spent long hours sitting on a bale of hay, watching sun motes dancing while the fragrance of the wild hedges bordering the fields moved lazily through the hot summer air. He tracked the smell, remembering how he'd been forced to find his own solace when he was growing up. Over time, his bitter memories began to weaken. They trembled with exhaustion and slowly moved aside for more tender memories.

He remembered being a little boy standing in sunbeams in the barn, rubbing his face in a horse's mane. He remembered the warm, soft feel of placid cows, and their flanks when he milked them. He remembered scuffing his big feet through pale, soft, tan, warm summer dust.

Slowly he started understanding that he'd always held the potential to be a happy, positive child, albeit a somber, large one. God forbid, maybe he might have grown into a sensitive, yet manly man. One thing might have led to the next.

But Fate had ordained a different path for him to walk. He began to understand and accept that something or someone bigger caused his life to be the way it was for reasons he might never know. But in the end, it would somehow come out right, and it would have something to do with the needy, dancing children that saved his soul.

Chapter 15. Red Boggs

Iron Ore
Rust

One day he went into town to pick up a package. He waited by the depot, idly watching passengers step off the train. A young red-headed boy stepped off the train. He looked to be about eleven years old. Tired and dusty, his clothes were too small. A thin gunny sack was slung across his shoulder.

He guessed the boy's few possessions were in the gunny sack. There were many orphan children trying to find homes around the country these days. Though he hadn't seen any around Cross Grove, he'd seen quite a few in Chicago.

One of the men unloading the train handed him his package. On impulse, he called to the boy to carry the package to the buggy, even though it was something he could have done easily. The boy studied him with uncertainty before he scuffed his way over to him.

He shoved the package into the boy's arms and strode to the buggy, the boy trailing him. He took the package from the boy and placed it in the buggy. He placed a coin in the boy's hand.

"If you can make your way out to my place, I got work for you." He gave the boy his name, directions to the farm, got in the buggy and drove away. He didn't look back at the red-headed boy.

After giving himself some heady praise on the way home, he realized his generous impulse had just got him in trouble. What was he going to do with someone else on the place? He cursed himself the rest of the way home, heartily hoping the boy wouldn't show up.

But he did. A knock on the door, several hours later. "He must have run to get here," he muttered to himself, opening the door.

The boy was skinny. His fine, carrot-colored hair was long and ragged. His white skin was that of a true redhead, and it was badly sunburned. Freckles ran across the bridge of his blunt, round nose. The boy watched him with unwavering blue eyes, his wide mouth curved down. The interrogation began.

"What's your name?"

"Red Boggs."

"You're an orphan?"

"Yes sir. I don't have no family or home no more. I lost them all in the epidemic in New York City. The hospital put me on the orphan train headed west."

Addition Jones had heard similar stories before. He put the boy to cooking while he hurried out to the barn, hastily dismantled his paint things and locked them away in the little back room.

Red Boggs stayed wary of him, but he loosened up after he ate all he could hold. He could tell the boy needed sleep. He made a mental note to get in more food supplies and assigned him Nell's old bedroom. The boy said little. He fell into a deep sleep as soon as his head touched the pillow.

Red was wiry and strong, a hard worker. He took it on himself to rise early in the morning, stoke up the kitchen stove and brew a pot of savory, hot coffee, just the way they both liked it. Then he made flapjacks and fried meat and eggs for their breakfast. He had large, capable boy's hands and big feet. Addition Jones made a mental note to get Red Boggs new shoes.

He couldn't paint. That was the problem. He didn't want Red Boggs to know anything about his private life, so he couldn't go to the little room in the barn and paint.

He'd cut himself off from the intense labor he loved. He stayed ornery and irritated. Day after day he walked the farm, trying to find a way to get rid of Red Boggs so he could regain his privacy, and go back to painting.

One day, out of the blue, the perfect solution came to him. It was so simple! He should have thought of it before! Why, he would just give Red Boggs to those people who called themselves his parents!

He went to town and bought the boy a new pair of work boots, handkerchiefs, underwear, tan pants, and a plaid shirt. At home, he handed the packages to the boy.

"Thanks, Mr. Jones," Red Boggs said, his face bright with pleasure as he opened the packages.

"You can wear them tomorrow when I take you over to stay with some people I know."

The look of pleasure faded from Red Boggs face. The boy looked at him and gulped, "Ain't I workin' hard enough for ye' to keep me?"

"It's not that," Addition Jones hastily improvised. "They need help." He floundered for words, surprised at the hurt look on the boy's face. "They're old, and they need your help more than I do," he improvised. The boy's face went pale, then dead white. He shrugged calmly, accepting his fate.

*

After a sleepless, guilt-ridden night, Addition Jones was on his way to see his parents. In the back of his wagon, carelessly wrapped, lay the picture of his grandfather. He had no use for it. He planned to give it back to them, along with the boy.

He glanced over at Red Boggs. He'd followed the orphan boy around, explaining over and over that the people he would be living with were old and sorely needed a good farm hand. He'd stammered and stuttered, wishing to hell that the A.J. Jones whom Chicago businessmen dreaded, was back in a boardroom where he ran the show, not following an orphan boy around, apologizing to him.

"I just don't have enough work for you on my place," he protested. Red Boggs never looked him square in the eye again. He just shrugged in answer.

Addition Jones drove into their yard and stopped. He watched Nola step out on their wide, shady porch. She wiped her hands on a dish towel and shaded her eyes with her hand. He watched her body jerk in surprise when she realized it was him. Satisfied with her reaction, he announced to her from the wagon, "I brought you a boy to help around the place. His name is Red Boggs, and I got him at the train station in Cross Grove. He's an orphan boy and a good worker. If you can't use him, then give him to somebody else."

Red Boggs sat perfectly still, looking straight ahead, his freckles standing out on his white face. Addition Jones nudged him, and he climbed down from the wagon. He stood there with his gunny sack in one hand, the other hand clinging to the wagon wheel.

Nola looked at the scared boy with bright red hair and the freckled, white face underneath it. His longing blue eyes stared back at her, bright with fear. The wagon began to move away. Her son was trying to get away!

Shocked and dismayed, Nola shouted at him, "What are you doing? You can't give people away! That boy's scared to death! And now you're running away, you mean, spiteful coward!"

Her words caught him off guard. They stung and hurt him. HE was mean? HE was a coward? Who the hell did she think she was?

"We've had to live with losing you, but you don't have to, huh? Trying to send us a replacement, so you can shut us out of your life again?" she shouted at him.

"Hah!" he shouted in reply. Enraged, he whirled the wagon around. Red Boggs jumped out of his way.

"Jason!" Nola screamed, looking towards the barn. Jason came running out of the barn and intercepted him. He grabbed the horse's harness and pulled the wagon to a stop.

Jason stood there, stopping him from leaving. He was huffing and puffing, but he spoke calmly, "So, it's you! Decided to visit us, did you?"

Addition Jones didn't answer. Suddenly he felt ashamed of himself.

"Get out of the wagon," Jason ordered. Nola ran down the steps to Jason's side.

"He brought this poor, scared orphan boy here, and tried to drop him off!"

She pointed to Red Boggs with tears in her voice. Thunderstruck, Jason looked at her, at Red Boggs, and then back at him. Addition Jones watched his father's face darken with anger.

"First things first."

Jason looked at Red Boggs.

"Take him in the house and feed him. Tell him he can stay with us, not to worry. I want to have a word with our son."

Nola hesitated.

Jason said, "Don't worry. He won't leave without telling you goodbye."

Addition Jones felt a flush of shame as Jason gave him a hard look. The old man stood silent and waited until Red Boggs trailed Nola into the house. When they were out of sight, Jason turned to him.

"What the hell do you think you're doing?"

Addition Jones reached past his shame and found his anger. It felt comfortable.

"Just brought a boy to work for you," he muttered sullenly.

"You fool!" Jason hissed. "You can't replace yourself with us! You can't bring us a boy to take the place of you! He's a human being! You can't give people away! Thought you'd scare somebody like you got scared, huh? Get out of that damn wagon and stand on the ground you belong on and be damn glad I don't give you a licking for trying to do that to another lost child!"

It was either run over his father or get out of the wagon. It was amazing how he reverted to being a child here on his folks' farm. Where was the A.J. Jones who was the scourge of every boardroom in Chicago? He climbed down from the wagon and glared at Jason. Up close, they were even more alike; they were the same height. They looked each other in the eye; tall, rough, dark, big-knuckled men. Addition Jones was glad he'd chosen not to fight Jason.

"You're going to take a little walk with me," Jason commanded, his eyes snapping with decision.

"Come on!" he ordered. He turned and began to walk off. Addition Jones sighed. He trailed along behind his father, slowly realizing what a bad idea this had been.

"Alexander Jason Mennebar. That's your real name," Jason said, tossing the curt words back over his shoulder at him.

"Someday, this place will be yours, and none of us have any time left to waste on hardened pride or self-pity over what life has handed us!"

He didn't hear the rest of Jason's lecture. *Alexander Jason Mennebar. His real name.* He repeated it over and over to himself. *Alexander Jason Mennebar. A.J. again. Only better. No more Addition Jones! Never again!* He realized he was giving in. He reached deep inside and found a resentment.

"The boy that fit that name didn't grow up here. I got my own place. Give your damned place to somebody else."

Jason turned and glared at him.

"First of all, you need a good smudging!"

He didn't dare ask Jason what a "smudging" was.

"Second of all, this place is not damned. Neither is yours, not anymore, only because of Nell. Third, yes, you've already got a place, but I ask you, what kind of place is it, and what have you got plenty of on it besides misery and hate? What is its future? Is it going to help somebody someday? If you've been given a farm to take care of by the Earth, then you owe the Earth to treat it right. All Travelers know that! You have to plan for its future, for that part of Earth has put itself in your hands. It wouldn't have, if you didn't have something to offer it, some sort of vision for it.

It's time you grew up and acted like a man and stopped putting the blame on us for what happened to you. We didn't do it! And you best leave off thinking about getting petty revenge on us or anybody else. Take this second chance at life while you've still got it!"

With the last withering dregs of his anger, Addition Jones gestured towards the house

"Maybe she should have watched me better."

Jason watched his son bow his head. He knew he must be feeling like his soul was under fire. He sighed and spread his big hands on his hips, searching for patience, his legs planted apart like they were growing down into the earth.

"Your mother suffered a nervous breakdown after you were kidnapped. You were a baby, sleeping in a basket out in the back yard when it happened. She was hanging up clothes. She ran short of clothespins and went into the house to get some more. She took them off of some skirts. When she came back, you were gone, but she didn't know it.

You were a quiet baby, so she didn't think anything about it. When she finished hanging up the clothes, she checked the basket and found a rock under the covers instead of you. She realized you'd been kidnapped and she lost her mind."

Jason shrugged.

"We hired detectives to find you and the kidnapper. She set in a chair by the front window for over a year, watching the road, waiting for someone to bring you back, while I let the farm go to hell, and stayed out searching for you. I almost lost her. Her mind was gone for that time. I took good care of her like she took good care of you, and she came back to me, in time. Thank God I didn't lose you both."

Jason shook his big, thick finger at his son and said, "So, don't you be mean to her; she can't take it. I won't risk losing her again. Do you understand me?"

"Why did Grady Miller do it?"

Jason sighed and said, "Who knows? He met Nola and told her he was a single man. She went for him for a little while because of his wild ways. She's a Traveler, and she thought he matched her fire. She was attracted to his beauty and passion; we Travelers are always attracted to those things! Then she found out he was a married man. His passions were poisoned.

She told him to leave her alone, but he wouldn't. She stayed afraid of him; by then she realized how crazy and mean he was. That's when I came into the picture. We were friends long before any of that ever happened. He left her alone after we were married, and we both thought it was over.

We never suspected him. We never knew if you were dead or alive until Nell wrote us. Nola would have killed Grady Miller, and I would have helped her, but he was already in his grave. From what I heard about him, you're lucky he left you alive. There is that to be thankful for. Grady Miller, the Smiths and that town you live in have plenty to answer for someday. But it's not our job to see to that."

Jason frowned at him and put his hands on his hips. He said, "Now, you brought this boy over here, but he can't take your place. We will keep him here to spare him from your ignorance and cruelty, because you don't know how to act right now."

He waited while his son turned his back to him, fighting for control of his emotions. He finally turned to Jason and speaking with disguised calm, said, "Well, that's enough for today. I'm leaving now."

"Nola!" Jason shouted, without taking his eyes off his son. "You didn't think you were going to run away without saying goodbye to your mother, did you?"

Nola ran down the steps towards them.

*

Alexander Jason Mennebar, A.J., no longer known to himself as Addition Jones, managed to hold it all in until he was out of sight of their farm. Then he pulled the wagon over and let it go.

All kinds of noises poured out of him. Shrieks and shouts and new words mixed with snorts and laughter. His real mother had hugged him! His first hug from his own mother! He would never forget how it felt!

Hot tears poured down his thin cheeks, etching salty red trails in his swarthy skin. His legs trembled and he was glad he was sitting in the wagon. When the emotional storm was over, he drove home.

He left them Red Boggs, a boy who needed them like he once needed them. He knew they would love Red Boggs like he couldn't. He had been scolded and embraced and he was carrying home his real name and his birth date. It was all he could stand for now. He just wanted to get home and start painting again!

Chapter 16. The Way of Paint

Risk Management
Water

Nell heard that Addition Jones recently picked up an orphan boy at the train station. The town suspected he was forcing the boy to stay out on his farm, working him to death, not feeding him, making him live out in the barn.

Nell's rage grew. *Why not? He was absolutely capable of making the boy live out the same life he himself endured! He probably didn't think anything was wrong with it!* The town could just talk and not do anything about it this time too, but she would put a stop to it!

She shuddered at the secret memories of the horror she once suffered at his hands and made a quick decision. She would go out to the farm and bring the boy home with her!

*

She flew out to his farm, dust whirling through the air behind her buggy. She whipped the buggy into the yard, jerked it to a stop, and jumped out.

A.J., as he thought of himself now, had just finished stabling the horse from taking Red Boggs to his parent's house. He would never use his old name again, the ridiculous one assigned to him by two evil old bastards! He had a good start on it, for he was already known as A. J. Jones everywhere but here.

She watched him, hands on hips. He was on his way out of the barn carrying a towel and something in his hands. She didn't notice or care what it was. He set whatever it was down on the board laying across the end of the water trough by the corral and turned to her. He watched her advance towards him, fists clenched.

"Are you keeping an orphan boy out here?" she shouted. "Have you murdered him yet? Is he still alive? Where is he? You understand, don't you, that you will not put him through the kind of hell you grew up in? That will never happen to another child again if I can help it!"

He stared at her. So that's what the people in town were saying. An old familiar weariness welled up in him. Now was not the time for this clash; he'd been through enough today.

He watched her pace back and forth, yelling, working herself into a frenzy. He wasn't inclined to say a word to stop her, or to defend himself. He seemed to be guilty of a lot of things today.

Suddenly she bent over, grabbed a small stone and threw it at him. Reflexively, he ducked. She picked up another stone and threw it at him with all her might.

"The people in town think you plan to murder that orphan boy and bury him somewhere on this property! That's how much they think of you! I know you're crazy because of what you've done to me and I'm here to take him away from you before you hurt him, too!"

"He's not here. I took him to those people you sent out here."

She didn't hear his words. She was busy yelling and throwing stones at him. He held his ground and kept on ducking the small stones; he let out a short, involuntary groan when one of the stones hit him particularly hard. She heard the little groan and stopped.

He was surprised her words and stones hurt him; even more surprising, he couldn't stop the hurt from happening.

"Damn it!" he shouted in frustration. She'd picked a hell of a time to show up. Just when the carefully built defenses around his heart were crumbling. Just after he dropped off Red Boggs.

He turned inward from her scathing words to peer past the smooth, soft bird down, past the prickly quills he'd protected his weary heart with. He realized he'd begun to hope, secretly and in a big way. Now, that hope stood in front of him, throwing rocks at him, wishing him dead.

A piercing awareness flooded him. She was old, he was old, and here they stood, fighting, just like her father predicted! He turned away from her in defeat and lurched crookedly towards the barn.

She stood there panting, another rock in her hand. In the instant before he turned away, she saw the tremendous pain in his black eyes. She watched his thin, long mouth go trembling and soft. In her mind, she heard the soft little groan of pain escape him while she hurt him again and again in the silence of the farmyard.

Remorse welled up in her. Her anger fled. Great tearing sobs of pity for both of them wrenched their way out of her. She didn't know what to do next. She looked this way and that. As if she was deflated, with nothing left inside her, she sank to the ground. She covered her face and mouth with her hands and sobbed like he did earlier.

He stopped and turned around. She cried until her eyes were so swollen she could barely see before she was done. The pins holding her hair in place were gone. Her hair hung straight and loose down her back.

She wanted to leave, but she knew she couldn't go back to town looking like she did. They would think some awful thing happened to her and start even more gossip! She sifted through the dust with her fingers and found a few hairpins. She looked around and saw the water trough with the wash pan and towel sitting on the board across the end of it.

At least she could wash her face and cool it off so it wouldn't be so red. She got up and staggered over to the horse trough. She dipped her hands into the cool water over and over, splashing her eyes and hot, flushed face.

She smoothed her hair back with her damp hands. With closed eyes, she fumbled for the towel and wiped her face, pinned up her hair, and headed for the buggy. She climbed into the buggy and started to drive away. She felt reasonably clean and presentable. She would take her time driving back to town to give her eyes and face a chance to cool down, she reasoned.

*

He watched her stop crying, stand up and stumble over to the water trough. He watched the sun pick out the silver in the long, straight hair hanging down her back. He watched her rinse her face, smooth her hair back, then search for the towel with closed, swollen red eyes. He watched her hands fumble across the fresh paint palette he'd set down on the board beside the towel when she drove into the yard.

He watched her lift her hands, filled with smears of fresh oil paint from the palette and wipe her face and hair with them. He watched her closed eyes and listened to her deep sighs and the little hiccups of air. He watched while she smeared more water and paint over her face and hair.

He was utterly enthralled. The artist in him was fascinated and stood back, watching one of women's oldest rituals take place. The more paint she smeared on herself, the more beautiful she became. Unaware of what she was doing, she turned into an ancient, primal woman engaged in the timeless ritual of painting herself. She changed into a woman belonging to Nature alone, owned by it, beautiful and powerful and terrible.

He almost called out to warn her about the paint; he suspected he was already in big trouble, not for the first time this day.

"Will this damned day never end!" he muttered, cursing to himself, wishing he was the terror of a boardroom, any boardroom, anywhere, happily intimidating people within an inch of their lives.

He told himself he should stop her, tell her what she was doing to herself, but he froze at the thought of her attacking him again. And how to explain the paints? What would someone like him be doing with expensive oil paints?

He waited until she got in her buggy. Until it was his last chance to stop her. She would never be able to explain the paint to herself or the town if he let her leave. He ran across the yard and grabbed her horse's bridle.

She gave a violent start and clutched the reins tighter. He held his grip on the bridle and stated matter-of-factly, "You have paint all over your face and hair." He didn't know what else to say. She glared at him like he was a liar and ran a slow finger down her face. It came away with streaks of teal blue paint on it. She stared at it open-mouthed.

"The paint was on the... umm...board by the towel." He shut up. She looked at him. He knew better than to say anything more.

She threw up her hands helplessly and rolled her swollen, reddened eyes up to heaven. She couldn't possibly go back to town looking like she apparently did. The town would be talking about it for the next hundred years! And she could never tell them what happened. It was none of their business that she'd gone running off to throw little pebbles at the big man who was the greatest source of shame for everybody in town. She would lose her hard-won place in the town's social structure, and probably all of her dress clients too!

He waited, studying the tragic thoughts running across her red-eyed, swollen face while she figured it out. He knew what she was thinking, and he just couldn't help smirking at her. He knew it would make her mad all over again, but what the hell. It was just going that way today!

He thought about inviting her in to clean the paint off, but was too afraid of her finding his books and other private, gentlemanly things in the house. Hell, she might die of shock at the Beast-man owning partially refined gentleman's things. And what would the town do to him if they found yet another dead body...hers...even if it was natural causes...on his property?

She interrupted his thoughts.

"All right! How do I get it off? Get me a mirror!" she ordered as she clumsily climbed back out of the buggy. She stood there glaring at him, waiting, the paint on her face making her look like a primitive woman setting out on a kill.

"Ahhh...Ahhh... I guess I will have to clean it off you?" he questioned carefully.

She glared at him while the world spun on its axis. "It's oil paint. Water won't clean it off. It will require linseed oil and a few other things to remove it," he explained. "I'll bring everything out to the water trough."

She glared at him and spoke stiffly. "I'll need a mirror, soap, and a comb too!"

He sauntered to the house. Once inside, he hastily grabbed an ivory-handled mirror, comb, a huge, fluffy white towel and a bar of French milled soap. He stopped in the kitchen to collect the new wash basin and matching pitcher. He remembered to saunter when he went back out the door carrying everything.

He set the collection of items on the board by the water trough. Then he sauntered to the barn to get the linseed oil and other things he needed from his little room.

She stood by the water trough waiting, painted, angry, watching his every move. Nonchalantly, he poured a tiny bit of linseed oil on a clean cloth and advanced towards her. Unwillingly, she held her chin up to him and closed her eyes.

He stood as far back from her as he could, reached forward, and gingerly dabbed the cloth on her chin. That part worked. But the rest wouldn't. He would have to hold her face to do it. When his long, bony fingers touched her, she flinched but didn't pull away. The paint came off smoothly from everywhere he touched.

He looked her over. Nell Miller. He instinctively knew this opportunity would never happen again in his lifetime. He repeated her name in his mind as he gently touched linseed soaked cloth to a streak of jet-black paint. The black of a crow's wing.

Another streak of purple oil paint lay in the fine silver hair near her left temple. Purple for the lilacs blooming behind the crow. He felt her breath waft across his wrist. He knew she felt his breath moving across her forehead and ears. Her ears were shaped like large, pale pink seashells. She and water belonged together. Had she ever seen the ocean? Her forehead held the long shape of intelligence, the lines of a deep thinker. There were many lines in it; he entertained the peculiar thought that maybe he should count them.

He stopped his mind from going where it was headed and finished cleaning the paint off her face. Her eyes were still closed, the paint was gone, but he kept dabbing as though there was a bit more paint here and there.

He looked at the lines around her eyes and mentally traced the shape of them with his fingers. He regarded her sparse, delicate, long gray eyelashes, her straight, prissy long nose, and her long, straight, bossy mouth with dimpled corners. He ran his thumbs across her sharp, high cheekbones, and heard her intake of breath. Her eyes stayed shut, but her cheeks flooded with color; her chin jutted out in an attitude of defiance as if she were saying, "I dare you."

He told himself he was just looking at her as an artist. After all, he was a sort of artist now. A.J. the artist, He felt like shouting with laughter.

*

She anticipated feeling revulsion when he touched her, but his touch was as dry, innocent and clumsy as it was diligent and searching. She knew he would not leave a spot of paint untouched. He was a thorough man. She could feel his breath brushing her forehead as he worked. She'd forgotten how tall he was. With a wry set to her mouth, she felt the back of her hair. Her hand came away with red paint on it. Red for a cardinal.

"You'll have to clean the paint out of the back of my hair, too," she ordered. She turned her back to him and waited.

He poured a tiny bit of linseed oil on a clean cloth and touched it to her hair. He never realized her hair was so long. Although she was tall, the top of her head was just under his chin.

He kneaded oil into her hair with his fingers, then rubbed the paint out with a clean white cloth. He felt the soft, straight strands slipping through his fingers over and over. They felt like silk.

He worked until all the paint was gone. At last, he stepped back. The sun was suddenly too hot; his ears were ringing.

"It's done," he said.

She turned around, her gray eyes wide as the doves he remembered, and stared at him. He held her look with his black eyes. Violins sang sharply in high notes, flooding his blood while his heart harkened back to another, darker time. They stared at each other solemnly, thinking similar thoughts. What just happened?

Neither knew. But the Fates knew. The Ritual was completed. Their Fates stood in the yard, silently laughing at them. They'd tricked the Beast into painting Beauty into his Light, and she accepted the Ceremony. They had both been tricked again!

Abruptly he turned away, tossing words back over his shoulder. "All done, Nell. You'll have to wash the linseed oil out. The soap and towel are right there."

She started in surprise, staring after his retreating back. He'd called her by name. She watched him walk into the barn and close the door. She supposed he walked away to give her privacy.

She picked up the bar of soap and sniffed it. She detected a faint scent of lemongrass. Then she smoothed the fluffy, snow-white towel and picked up the ivory-handled mirror. Him owning these kinds of things made no sense.

She unbuttoned the top two buttons of her dress, rolled her sleeves up past her elbows, washed her neck and throat and arms. She leaned over the water and washed her hair with the fragrance of the expensive soap wafting in the air around her.

The combination of the fluffy, exquisite towel, the scented soap, the heat of the sun and the quiet, natural space surrounding her felt so good she wanted to climb into the water trough and let her skin soak up the warm water and the sunshine. She looked around. Once upon a time this was her place.

She claimed it back for a few minutes by sitting on the round, metal lip of the water trough, the same trough she'd put there in the beginning. She sat, swishing her feet and legs through the water while her hair and dress dried in the sun.

In a short time, her hair was almost dry. The magic was over. It was his place again. She pulled her sleeves down, buttoned up the collar of her dress, pinned up her hair. She put her shoes and stockings on, climbed into the buggy, and drove out of the yard.

*

He sat on a bale of hay in the barn. Sunlit bars of light filled with dust motes floated around him while he imagined lathering her hair and rinsing it. He imagined the soft nape of her neck exposed to him, his fingers running along its length. He imagined the scent of the French milled soap on her.

He heard the buggy leave. Silence settled around him. He got up and unlocked the door to his childhood room and stepped inside.

He studied the richness of the painted birds filling the canvases and walls, waiting for the familiar anger, emptiness, hate, or resentment to show up to define his life. This time, none of them showed up to keep the Beast alive, even though he wasn't painting to keep them away. He was just standing there.

Instead, he felt the sinew and bone of himself resting and alive without any darkness. He felt and heard the rhythm of his blood moving through his veins beneath his flesh in a steady, smooth, rhythm. He snorted in surprise. Was he finally becoming who and what he was meant to be? A name and a birthday. More than paint was washed away this day. Gifts had been given. "Thank you," he muttered dryly to Red Boggs, his parents, Nell and the Fates.

He was damn near exhaustion. "It's been one hell of a day!" he muttered to himself. He could go no farther. He threw himself down on the little cot in his room and fell asleep.

*

Nell hurried home. Margaret was taking care of the ladies in their dressmaking parlor. She slipped through the back door, rushed to her room, re-pinned her hair, and changed into a fresh dress, the scent of the expensive French milled soap clinging to her.

When she walked in, Margaret lifted an eyebrow in silent question. Nell nodded and smiled, but gave no explanation. She sat down, averted her face and began sewing.

She'd rushed out to the farm, expecting something very different than what happened. She'd grabbed onto something she needed to exist, something no one else wanted, something despised and hated. It was bitter and black, and it squawked, but it brought her back to Life! It was dark bones and black rags, complaining skin and hard labor. It was as old as she was. It was as lonely as she was. It had done without the same things she'd done without. It knew the same deprivation, shame and dislike.

They'd always known each other; she'd discovered that this very day. He touched her for the second time, from a different place, and to her surprise, his touch was kind.

She'd keep her thoughts secret, for the townspeople hated and despised him. They would be shocked. No one but her was capable of loving or understanding him. She didn't understand it either; she didn't know what to do with it; she couldn't explain it to them anyway. She would hide it from them and protect it, whatever it took, whatever it cost. It was hers and none of their business.

A person had to have been as alone as the two of them before they could understand the place they'd met in today. He'd met her stoning with colors in beautiful paint, and now they stood together in the journey ahead. The Fates had decreed it. A small seed had been planted today. She would wait and let it grow into what it would without trying to stop it anymore.

Margaret noticed Nell's new confidence and felt her drawing away from her. She was puzzled and hurt. Something was hardening and cooling in Nell. Sometimes, she watched Nell staring out the window at nothing, her cheeks flushed with pale pink color, her long lips clamped down into a thin line of trembling determination.

Margaret watched the new confidence Nell displayed with people. She looked them in the eye and didn't look down or blush when someone talked to her. But she also didn't confide in her like she used to. That was the bad part. Margaret felt the loss of their old friendship keenly.

Chapter 17.   Family Ties

Radius
Root

He prepared the farm for winter. He weatherproofed the barn and other buildings. He sealed all the cracks everywhere. The feed and grain were in dry storage for the scant stock he kept. He cut and stacked the wood to heat the house in long, neat rows near the back door.

Inside the house, a large, thick navy and tan rug lay in front of the fireplace. Heavy tan and navy blue plaid drapes at the windows kept out the heat or cold. The living room was lined with filled bookshelves.

Two rockers sat near the fireplace. Large reading lamps, small polished wood tables and a long, navy blue sofa with generous pillows piled in the corners lined one wall. Plaid throws draped the back of the sofa and lay across the buttery soft leather of two large maroon chairs facing each other near the sofa.

He'd added a new indoor bathroom to the back of the house. The plumbers modified one of the new water pipe systems becoming popular in the city to fit his well water system.

The pantry was stocked with home canned chicken, wild game, pork, and beef, provided by a farmer and his wife from Benton. Sacks of beans, flour, salt and baking powder lined the pantry shelves next to tins of lard.

The bedroom sets were rich polished walnut. The king size beds were covered with deep blue quilts, white goose down pillows, and lofty feather beds. Heavy rugs in dark, intense colors edged each bed for bare feet to step on instead of cold wood floors.

His closet held new night slippers, boots, and thick robes. In his dresser were neat stacks of underwear and heavy wool socks. Plaid shirts and wool pants hung in neat rows in his closet. When he sent Baines, his personal assistant, a list of what he required for wintering at the house, Baines wrote back, asking him what color schemes to use.

He snorted in disdain. Ridiculous! He ordered Baines to choose for him. He ended up with manly tans, virile blue checks, and courageous reds. And he liked them.

It was nearly dusk when the first snow of winter started, drifting cautiously down in tiny flakes. He stood at a window watching, his thoughts on Nell. He hadn't seen her since the summer paint incident.

He shook his head. He couldn't have her around! Seeing her all the time would be a constant reminder of what her father did to him, and they would only hurt each other.

Anyway, the craziness he suffered with had left him that day. That's all that really mattered. He was only accountable to himself once again. He strolled over to a bookshelf, chose a book, and settled into his easy chair by the fire to read the collected works of H. Merriweather Throve, who believed a good murder mystery was the best thing in life.

Chapter 18. A Soul's Decline

Quadrant
Prime Number

Margaret glanced anxiously at the calendar again, then at the snow falling outside the kitchen window. It was the first of November. Snow was still falling, and Nell was still sick. Nell began feeling tired a few days ago, then a fever took over.

Margaret carried the cool, wet cloth back to the bedroom where Nell lay sleeping and sat down on the bed beside her. Nell didn't wake up. Margaret wiped her face gently and studied her, trying to figure out what to do. She was becoming desperate. Nell was getting worse. Her fever was climbing slowly and steadily. She was on the verge of delirium.

The veterinarian was the only doctor in Cross Grove, and he was out of town. The nearest medical doctor lived in Milford, a small town forty miles away. A desperate idea flashed through Margaret's mind. It could work. Maybe. She made a quick decision.

"Betsy, come sit with Nell! I'll be back as fast as I can!"

She jerked her coat on and rushed out of the house and down to the train station. She stood on the platform in the falling snow, waiting for the next train to pull in. A doctor might be on board.

At last the train arrived. Everyone got off to stretch their legs while the depot men unloaded the goods destined for Cross Grove. Margaret asked each passenger if there was a doctor on board. None of them knew.

She watched Addition Jones step off the train. He was wearing an expensive, finely cut dove gray overcoat, a dark blue muffler wound around his neck. His large hands were covered with black gloves. He walked past her without speaking. She ignored him and grabbed the coat sleeve of the man behind him.

"Are you a doctor?" she asked.

The man shook his head no and hurried away. Addition Jones stopped and turned around. He watched Margaret ask more passengers if they were doctors. He walked up to her, his black eyes boring into hers.

"Why do you need a doctor?"

"Because Nell is deathly sick, and the veterinarian is in Chicago for the holidays!" Margaret wailed, wringing her hands together in misery. He paled as his mind filled with fearful surprise. It never occurred to him that Nell wouldn't always be healthy and right where he needed her to be! He might have future plans for her. But that was supposed to be later, much later, not now!

He stood like a stone while Margaret rushed past him to ask the last of the passengers about a doctor. The conductor and ticket taker checked with everyone on the train. There was no doctor on board. His shock passed. His mind started functioning again, and he made a swift decision. He ran over to the men unloading the train.

"How much longer will you be?" he demanded.

"Another half hour or so," they answered sourly.

Margaret was still talking to the passengers from the train. He moved swiftly with purpose through the crowd, ignoring them, and grabbed her arm.

"Where is Nell?"

"At the boarding house."

"Come with me!" he commanded, and turned away. They hurried down the snowy street. He reached the boarding house, ran up the steps and crossed the porch. He jerked the door open and rushed in.

"Who's here?" he shouted.

Mrs. Ashley came out of Nell's bedroom. She backed up against the wall when she saw him. He ignored her silly reaction.

"Get Nell ready. I'm taking her on the train with me to find a doctor!"

Mrs. Ashley hesitated. Margaret spoke breathlessly from behind him.

"Hurry, Betsy! We haven't got much time! No doctor came in on the train. We're going to have to take her to Milford to the closest doctor! Tell Claude I'll call him later."

He'd stood enough! Impatiently he brushed past Mrs. Ashley and opened Nell's bedroom door. He strode to the bed and stood over her. He studied her. Her eyes were closed. Two high spots of fever flushed her cheeks. Her hair was spread out on a white pillow. She wore a chaste, high necked, long sleeved white nightgown. A mound of blankets and quilts covered her. He threw off the covers, wrapped the sheet and a quilt around her, and picked her up.

Margaret slipped Nell's house shoes on her feet and pulled a wool cap over her hair. Carrying Nell in his arms as though she weighed nothing, he strode out of the boarding house back to the train depot.

The train passengers gawked at him. He ignored them. Margaret shot him a grateful look as they climbed on the train. He waited, holding Nell in his arms, while she found them seats. When the porter came by, she asked him for a private room.

The porter took one look at Nell and led them to a room. The private room had wide, padded benches on each side serving as seats or beds, with a large window between. He laid Nell down on one of the benches and placed her head on the pillow Margaret handed him from the luggage rack. He sat down beside Nell and felt her forehead. Her skin was hot and tight. He was surprised at how frail she looked. She was light as a feather when he carried her to the train.

He stood up and shrugged out of his coat. The train started moving. He felt it jolt as they left the station and picked up speed. Before long, the porter returned with the water and towels he ordered. He tipped the porter, sent him away and turned to Nell. Margaret stepped forward to wipe Nell's face with the towel, but he warded her off with his hand. She watched him dip a snowy white washcloth in the water, wring it out, and bathe Nell's face with it.

He studied Nell's face with a fierce intensity. The time for playing games and not making decisions concerning their future was over.

Nell moaned in protest when the cool cloth touched her hot face. When he finished, he stood and pulled the shade up covering the window. He stared out into the inky darkness, his back to Margaret. She studied his broad back as he watched the snow swirling outside the rushing train. Instinctively, she knew he wanted privacy, so she moved to the other end of the seat facing the door.

*

Nell knew she was somewhere filled with pain, a place she didn't want to be. It was too hot and too cold, all at the same time. She longed for someone to get her out of the awful place she was stuck in. She knew who she longed for, but she couldn't remember their name. She stayed in that place for a long time, searching for them. At last, she felt the presence she longed for. It picked her up and surrounded her, holding and protecting her from something bad. Snowflakes fell on her hot face, then they were wiped away with a cool cloth. She drifted in and out of a fevered sleep.

A short time later, the porter knocked on the door and nervously informed them that the people on the train were spreading rumors about the sick woman. They wanted them off the train at the next stop; they were afraid the woman carried the plague.

Margaret watched Addition Jones ask the porter to tell the nice, concerned passengers they would remain in their stateroom and not come out until they got to Milford. That should take care of their worries. The porter nodded and left. The train rushed on through the night. Margaret studied him. He wasn't surprised by the porter's words. She wondered how often people misinterpreted his decisions and actions.

The porter came by later and announced the train would be pulling into Milford shortly.

He put on his coat and scooped Nell up in his arms. Margaret wrapped the quilt tighter around Nell and pulled the wool cap down over her hair. He asked Margaret to wind his muffler around Nell's neck and ears.

"Call me A.J.," he said to Margaret. She nodded.

"Jones," he added. She nodded again. Snow was falling when they stepped off the train. More was coming. A blizzard was due any time. He strode up to the depot man, holding Nell in his arms. The depot man blanched and fell back a step.

"I'm A. J. Jones. Where does the doctor live?" he demanded in an impatient voice.

"Third house on the left."

He pointed towards Main Street. Before the man could speak again, he turned away and strode through the falling snow under the lamplight, carrying Nell in his arms, Margaret hurrying along behind him.

The doctor's house was ablaze with lights. Margaret banged on the door while he waited on the steps holding Nell. He felt the heat of the fever radiating from her. The doctor answered the door. He took one look at the face of the tall man cradling the sick woman in his arms, and motioned them into the house. They followed him down a long hallway. They heard the sounds of a piano and laughter coming from another part of the house.

"Lay her down over there," he ordered. Margaret explained Nell's sickness while the doctor examined her. When he was done, he shook his head somberly at them.

*

Milford was three times the size of Cross Grove. He rented a ground floor suite of rooms for Nell and Margaret and a smaller suite for himself at the best of the three hotels in Milford. The doctor stopped by every day to check on the patient. Through the doctor, he hired attendants to care for Nell around the clock, for she was still so sick he was scared he might lose her.

Claude took care of business back in Cross Grove while Margaret stayed in Milford to tend Nell, for Nell could not be left alone under the care of a man who wasn't her husband or a close relative. It just wasn't done. They would be forced to leave Milford if Margaret didn't stay on as chaperone.

Margaret held back tender, surprised laughter as she watched him handle every little detail having to do with Nell with the intensity of a person making life and death decisions. Packages filled with beautiful things for Nell arrived regularly at the hotel. Margaret watched him pull a long sable coat out of one of the boxes.

"This will keep her warm when she is better and wants to go outside again," he explained gruffly. A matching hat, muff, and supple gloves quickly piled up on the bed. Other boxes contained the most chaste, beautiful white cotton nightgowns Margaret ever saw.

*

Nell moved slowly back into life. She ate small amounts of food when urged. She sat in the chair by the window in the evening and stared out at the snow. The shades and curtains were kept drawn during the day because she couldn't stand the light.

The attendants helped her dress each morning. They did most of it for her because she had no interest in it. She simply indicated to them what she wanted, then lost interest and went back inside of herself to wherever it was she was living.

They clad her in the finest, simply designed clothes. They brushed her hair and rolled it into an uncomplicated bun and fastened it at the nape of her neck. Sometimes they wondered what she was thinking and tried to draw her out, but all she gave them was blank stares.

The attendants nodded knowingly to each other whenever "he" or the other "she" wasn't around. They'd heard the stories being spread around Milford saying the woman they were tending was kidnapped and brought to Milford by Mr. A. J. Jones and his female accomplice.

None of them liked his looks or manners. He spoke to them in a curt voice that brooked no argument. But, the money he paid them was much more than they could get anywhere else and their duties were light, so they smiled and spoke pleasantly to him.

Thanksgiving came and went. Milford decked itself out for Christmas. Streetlamps glowed. Carols filled the air. Nell's temperature was gone, but she was thin and pale and listless and didn't seem to care if she got better or not. The doctor took Addition Jones and Margaret aside.

"She has a spiritual malaise of some sort. She needs months of quiet and rest under comfortable conditions to heal her nerves, which I believe were broken somehow. She's going to need attendants, good food and fresh air, and if she gets better at all, she will most likely need to live with someone, at least for a long time, if she's to survive this breakdown. Best if she could live out in the country for a while."

His voice became businesslike, for he had other cases to tend to.

"Someone is going to have to take care of her for a long time, that's all there is to it. If she has enough money, you may be able to provide attendants for her in a private setting, but if she doesn't," he shook his head, "it means a state institution of some kind."

*

Margaret paced the floor, Claude's letter in hand. He needed her, and she missed him terribly. He wanted her to come home and bring Nell. He couldn't leave because of the store. It was their living. She thought about the situation. The doctor said Nell would be ill for a long time, maybe permanently. No one knew how long it would take her to get better, if she ever did.

She'd been gone much longer than she'd anticipated, but propriety dictated she stay to protect Nell's reputation, to keep A. J. Jones' attentions respectable and legal. Margaret thought it over. She would just have to take Nell back to Cross Grove and hire someone to help with her.

Margaret explained the dilemma to him.

"I have to go home, but I'll take her with me. You've certainly seen to her care."

She thought of the many times she ignored the attendants gossiping behind their hands.

"You can't stay here anyway. I'm sure you've heard the gossip making the rounds."

He nodded.

"She's going to stay here with me," he stated.

Margaret protested. "You can't stay with her, here or at home! It just isn't done. It would ruin her reputation. You of all people should know how other people are about those things!"

"She's not going with you. We'll get married."

Margaret blinked and stared at him in surprise. He paced back and forth, hands behind his back, his dark face averted.

"If I marry her, she will continue to have the best of care, just like she does now. The tongues can stop wagging, and she can get well in peace."

He glanced at Margaret and shrugged.

"Don't worry. I'll leave her alone. She hates me, so that's not a problem."

"Then why would you do it?"

He gave her a thin smile.

"Because it seems to be necessary."

*

The doctor agreed wholeheartedly when the situation was explained to him. With him on the bandwagon, no one else in Milford dared stand against them. Margaret smoothed the way for the wedding with judicious use of common sense and money provided by A.J.

Jones. She explained the situation to Nell, but Nell didn't seem to understand or care.

The marriage ceremony took place in the parlor in Nell's suite of rooms on Christmas day. Nell sat in the chair by the window, clad in a new blue dress. She nodded in response to the vows. The attendants stood up with the bride. They had been "gifted" with money for fine, new dresses they could never have afforded on their own.

Margaret wasn't surprised when A. J. Jones calmly gave his legal name as Alexander Jason Mennebar during the wedding ceremony. Now Nell would be Mrs. Alexander Jason Mennebar, instead of Nell Miller.

The small, white frosted wedding cake with pink flowers was cut and shared by the participants. Everyone made pleasant small talk for a short time before they hastily hurried home to their own Christmas. The next morning, Margaret boarded the train back to Cross Grove.

Chapter 19. Spring

Long Division
Loans

It was spring on the farm by the time he drove into the yard with Nell beside him. He felt the emptiness of the buildings, but the grass was newly green and hopeful, and pale shoots of flowers were peeking up around the house. He glanced at Nell to see if she noticed anything, but she just stared straight ahead, her hands motionless in her lap.

He climbed down from the buggy and stretched. It was good to be home. He opened the barn doors and stepped inside. It smelled sweet and quiet. He walked to the back of the barn, glanced at the padlocked door of his old room and breathed a small sigh of relief. It was still intact. He strolled back out into the sunlight to help Nell down from the buggy.

*

During the months in Milford, Nell's days and nights passed smoothly and steadily, without a ripple to disturb them. She observed Margaret crying and Addition Jones' black eyes peering down intently at her, trying to search out the place she inhabited now. She wasn't worried, even though there were no directions telling how to get there or how to return.

Through the window of an unfamiliar room, she watched snow falling on a strange street filled with lit streetlamps. Nothing mattered. Women in starched white dressed her and gave her food. She heard everything they said. She heard herself answering them, telling them not to worry, that she was all right. But she never spoke the words out loud. That was too hard to do.

Memories drifted in and out in pieces while she languidly observed all the parts of her life. She liked the pictures of her mother and the old farm where she grew up. She watched chickens peck and scratch the ground; she swung on the rope swing in the tree. She sang little songs while her hair flew out behind her. She climbed the pear tree and ate pears and tossed the cores down to the bees and birds waiting for them. She roamed the farm and slept in the barn when it rained. But she never went in the house, except to her mother's bedroom to brush her mother's hair and talk about sewing or storing vegetables.

There was no past or future, just a steady stream of days following each other. She was rich in the silence flowing around her. She felt like a feather floating in a stream, a tiny part of a life bigger than she ever imagined. She was content, taken care of.

*

Summer. She looked around. He'd brought her rocking chair back to Cross Grove with them on the train. She thought about that and looked up into his face, calmly studying the harsh planes as he bathed her in the horse trough by the corral. The hot sun felt good on her wet skin. The water was warm. She felt it soaking into her pores. He was practiced at bathing her now. His big hands moved smoothly over the chemise covering her. A glimmer of amusement flickered through her at the memory of the first few times he bathed her. He swore under his breath and handled her like she was an egg that might break any second. Suddenly a memory of him washing teal blue paint off her face flew into her mind. She frowned in puzzlement.

He took her hands in his, pulled her to a stand, and helped her step out of the water. She stood there waiting, her chemise clinging to her in the hot sun. Mrs. Thorn would be here in a minute to give her a massage.

He wondered. Was she young or was she old? He didn't know. He usually pinned her hair up into a soft ball on top of her head. Her hair quickly turned to silver this past winter.

He picked up the pail of rinse water and poured it slowly over her bowed head.

Mrs. Thorn whipped her buggy past him and stopped at the house. She shook her head and muttered sourly, "What's coming to this world! That man is a fool!"

There he was, bathing Nell in the horse trough again, right out in the hot sun.

"Indecent!" she muttered under her breath. "If it wasn't for the money he pays me, I'd turn around and never come back!"

She descended from the buggy and marched up the porch steps without a backward glance. She laid her hat and purse on the chair by the front door. Her eyes raked over the living room with contempt. Books everywhere. The shelves couldn't hold them all. She snorted and walked over to peer down at several of the open books on the floor. They were all about new-fangled methods of healing, like bathing in the sun.

She snorted. Well, nothing could help that woman! Not as long as she was with him, married or not! She stalked into Nell's bedroom, jerked a stack of crisp, snowy white sheets out of the closet and set to work.

First, she unrolled the pad that went on what he called the massage table. She slapped the pad down on the long thin table and covered it with a fresh, clean sheet. Next, she moved to Nell's bed, stripped it down and remade it. Then she tidied up the nightstand before she went to the kitchen to heat the oil for the massage she would be giving Nell.

Nell's rocking chair stood in front of the living room windows. The sun poured through the windows and warmed the cushions on the chair. One of her jobs was to fluff the cushions in Nell's rocking chair. Mrs. Thorn knew he put the chair there. She never knew where it would be. Sometimes it was on the porch or out in the yard.

*

Margaret stopped washing dishes and stared out the window over the kitchen sink. Things were different now. Claude's mother had passed away. She'd closed the dress shop. Now the boarding house was rented out to an older couple who took in boarders and cooked for them. They kept the place shipshape, respectable, and quiet.

The townspeople didn't liked A. J. Jones marrying Nell. They didn't like him living with her out on his farm. Gossip spread that he'd broken Nell's will to live and caged her up out on the old farm. Claude's patience with their meanness and foolishness was over. He snorted and barked out sharp words.

"Nonsense! Same song, endless verse, and all of them wrong! You know better!"

Margaret and Claude watched and waited in careful, protective silence for they knew Nell and A.J. were together for a good reason. Both had been alone, beset by evil since birth; both had lost their hope; both had fought evil alone since birth. But Fate had intervened in their lonely lives, and now they were married. At last they could fight evil's insistent return together.

They were perfect for each other, but the odds were stacked against them. Margaret and Claude believed that between them lay a great love waiting to be discovered.

Margaret's thought of Mrs. Thorn. Her mouth thinned down into a tight line. The woman was a malicious gossip, spreading lies about Nell and A. J. all over town. He was paying her a much larger salary than she deserved. Margaret set her mouth in grim determination. She would persuade him to hire a quiet farm woman she knew who took a much more natural view of life, a woman who knew how to keep her mouth shut.

Chapter 20. Discoveries

Long Term Division
Absolute Value

A. J. Mennebar strolled through the small, barren south pasture, remembering breaking up the rocks in it to ease his pain. He noticed a small, jagged chunk of broken rock gleaming in the sun, and picked it up. It fit the palm of his hand perfectly. He turned it over and studied the ribbons of bright gold streaked through with lovely pink color.

He put the rock in his pocket and handed it to Nell that night. She took the rock and examined it, then positioned it on the floor beside her chair. He picked it up and placed it on the fireplace mantel and promptly forgot about it.

*

Something inside Nell was stirring, insisting she move again. Her walk was shaky. She was using muscles not used in a long time. She ignored his pleased looks, walking more and more, holding the pink and gold rock in her hand.

She wouldn't walk without it. She didn't know why she was walking; it didn't matter. She was just doing it. The hot summer days flowed by as she observed how easy it was for her to become strong again.

He hovered near the barn, pretending he was repairing a leather harness so he could watch her the first time he saw her walking around the yard. She held the piece of pink rock he'd given her, staring intently at it, moving it around so it sparkled in the sunlight.

After a while, he grew used to her walking every day. He left her to wander around as she would while he went on with his work. From time to time he checked on her to see what she was doing.

She wandered everywhere on the farm. If the flowers needed watering, she walked past them. She didn't cook but needed the food he fixed. It was the walking that mattered to her.

The summer sun was hot. He pinned up her hair each morning before she went out. Sometimes he braided it and let it hang down her back. She refused to wear the sunbonnet he tried to put over it. She needed the sun, more and more of it.

She never crossed fences or opened gates or tried to remove any barriers standing in her way. She either walked around them or took another direction.

At first, she walked the fields close to the house. She rested under trees and in fence rows before she moved on, always carrying the pink and gold rock in her hand. As time went on, she roamed farther and farther away.

One day he came home to an empty house. He was hungry, and it was past the time he usually fixed their midday meal. On an impulse, he made two thick roast beef sandwiches, added a jug of cold water and a couple of apples, packed them in a basket and went to find her.

From then on, whenever he found the house empty at lunchtime, he filled the basket and carried it through the fields until he found her.

He watched her appetite and color improve. But she constantly fretted with her hair, moving her hands over it and pushing it back. And she dreamed at night. He heard her muttering in her sleep. He knew she was searching for a memory of something. He wondered what it was, and what would happen when it came back.

Margaret made Nell simple cotton sundresses to wear. The dress hems stopped at mid-calf so she could walk the fields easily in them. She stood Nell on a sheet of paper and drew the shape of her feet on it and A.J sent away for sandals and new shoes for her. He ordered them to be made of thin, soft leather with lightweight soles.

One day he packed the picnic basket and went to find Nell. She was close to the house. She followed him across the fields, dawdling along the way, stopping to look up at branches, listening to bird song.

On impulse, he headed for the small south pasture. He opened the gate and stood there, remembering the rocks breaking apart under his bitter fury. How sorry he'd felt for himself back then! It seemed so long ago! Back then he was parched, empty bones, a white skull dressed in hanging black. He'd been burning heat, trying to pour itself out into a hollow space that never existed. He'd lived with no place of rest. He'd been a fiery oasis of white chalk raging, roaming this farm.

But without that fury, he never would have broken the rocks open and discovered the pink, sparkling loveliness hidden inside them. He shrugged. Maybe rage had its uses.

The broken rocks lay sparkling in the sun. Nell moved past him, looked down at the rock she held in her hand, then at the rock piles in the barren field. She wandered through the pasture, examining them.

He found a grassy, flat place, spread the blanket out, and set the picnic basket down. When everything was ready, he called her. After they ate, she stretched out on the blanket and dozed off. He sat still for a long time before he eased his tall body up from the blanket. He stood there swaying, staring down at the broken pink and gold rocks and then at Nell.

His changed heart lay in this field among scattered, shattered pink and gold pieces of rock. She was his now; he had given his pink, shattered heart to her. He would never let her go again.

A cloud crossed the sun, dimming the sparkle of the rocks. The dark, hidden part of him surfaced, and for an instant, he hoped she would never speak again, except in her sleep. Then she would have to depend on him forever! He stared down at her with heart and soul vying for places on his dark face. Nell opened her eyes and stared up at him. She watched the emotions warring on his face.

For a long moment, they stared at each other while the protective shell she was living in silently shattered to pieces. She wanted to keep on taking from him and never look back. She wanted to stay in her shell. She never wanted to speak again. The rewards were great. She didn't have to hurt, and he was at her beck and call. Maybe it could last the rest of her life. All she needed to do was stay the way she was right now. Helpless and broken.

He broke the look and turned away. He gathered the picnic things and put them in the basket. It wouldn't do for her to know what he was thinking.

She stood, stepped off of the blanket, and watched him fold it. The horror of her thoughts prickled her skin, making it damp and clammy.

Her walks changed. She'd had a close call. Her unspeaking, indulgent pleasure became spare and lean. She was forced to stay guarded with him. She was already speaking again, but only when she was alone. He didn't know that a few days ago, she'd exclaimed out loud over a pretty bird she saw in a field.

She walked and talked out loud in the back fields and thought about her life. Summer would be over soon. Then fall would come. Then winter.

She frowned to herself. He wore a look of satisfaction on his face when he looked at her, and she couldn't help but see that Margaret was becoming less of a friend to her and more of a helper in his plans.

Margaret wouldn't protect her from him. Neither would anyone else, because he saved her life and married her. She supposed she should think of him as her knight in shining armor, but she couldn't.

She walked and made plans. She needed her money to leave. There was more than enough to leave in the bank in town. How to get it out was the problem, and how to get away from him long enough to get it. She drifted through the summer without finding an answer.

Chapter 21. The Shadow's last Dance

Calendar Days
Yearly Capacities

Margaret believed the old Nell would never return; that Nell had been gone too long. She wondered if Nell would ever be able to take care of her own affairs again. There was the farm Nell told her about and the money she transferred to the bank from where she used to live. The more Margaret thought about it, the more worried she became. She decided to talk to A. J. about the problem. Maybe he didn't know about the money and farm Nell inherited.

Nell picked a random flower here and there from the flowerbeds in front of the house, listening intently while Margaret stood by her buggy talking to him. She hid her outrage while they discussed her money and property as though she wasn't even there.

She walked quickly behind the house to hide the feelings showing on her face. She moved faster and faster until she was running. She hid on the knoll and watched him search for her after Margaret left. Time was running out. She needed a plan.

He watched her over the dinner table that night. Something was wrong. His senses were alerted. She knew he would watch her even more closely from that day on. She might as well begin.

She spoke slowly, "I want to go see Margaret."

The first words she'd said since her long illness fell heavily into the silence. He nodded, then looked away to hide his emotions. She watched his face. She saw the thoughts he didn't know she could see. There were dark shadows under his eyes. He stood up and left. She knew he was going out to the barn, to his little room, to think about her speaking again.

*

Bittersweet. It was bittersweet for both of them, he thought. *A new place for them to move into. She could not live without him. He knew it, but maybe she didn't. She needed him and he needed her. Her words were back again, and they would bring them together or drive them apart. He knew her words were planned. How long had she been back, not willing to speak, and why?*

*

Nell strolled down Main Street, her arm linked through Margaret's. People smiled and greeted them, but Nell could see the thin shades of judgment and hide-bound attitudes covering their thoughts. They believed she belonged to Mr. A.J. Jones. She was as much his as any of the stones on his farm. They took it for granted she liked it that way. Grimly, she set her plan in motion.

"Let's stop and visit Claude. I want to look at materials and ribbons."

Margaret nodded with delight. Nell searched through the rolls of ribbons until she found the largest, most expensive one. She took it to the counter and measured it out. Then she pretended to search through her purse for money to pay for the ribbon.

"I don't have enough money to pay for it. Would you set it back for me for a few minutes? I'm just going to step out and go to the bank. I'll be right back."

Margaret said, "We'll take care of it, Nell." She looked at Claude, and he nodded.

Nell smiled at her and said, "No, I want to do this myself."

She stepped towards the front door.

"Oh! And I might stop in at Mrs. Weavers to look at the hats after I go to the bank."

Margaret nodded, pleased, and turned to talk to Claude. Sweat dampened Nell's forehead as she measured her paces out of the store.

Steady. Not too fast. Look like you're not in a hurry, she told herself.

It seemed to take forever to draw her money out of the bank. The banker watched her with a question in his eyes but didn't try to stop her. She knew he wouldn't say no, because of the amount of money Mr. A. J. Jones kept on deposit in his bank. She placed the money carefully in the bottom of her purse.

She would have to leave town quick, before the banker told everyone she'd drawn all her money out. Then *he* would hear about it. She shuddered. She hurried back to the general store and paid Claude for the ribbon.

Back at the farm, she said to him, "Look at the pretty ribbon I got today."

He gave her a piercing look and replied, "Yes, I see it."

*

She stood under the tall oak tree on the knoll above the house, her hands dirty from digging. He was running an errand in town. After he left, she rushed to her room on winged feet, tugged her money from under the mattress, and fled out the back door.

She climbed the knoll, dug a hole underneath the small bush near the oak tree and buried the tin of money. She ran back down the hill, washed up and checked her dress and herself for any signs of dirt or disorder. Then she sat down in the rocking chair and picked up a book.

He loaded his supplies, left the wagon at the train depot, and headed down Main Street. Two men passed him, walking in the opposite direction. One of them threw words aimed at him back over his shoulder.

"Yep. That's what I heard. She took all her money out of the bank, and either she's gonna' build him another new house out there, or she's gonna use it to leave him."

He stopped dead in his tracks. He turned around to ask them what they meant, but the two men were hurrying out of sight.

Nell watched him unload the wagon. Something was wrong, but he didn't speak of it, and she dared not ask.

*

Summer was coming to an end. He rarely left the farm. He took his food and water with him to the fields, leaving her free to do as she pleased. She could have packed and left. He wouldn't discover she was gone for hours. There was plenty of time to walk to town, to catch the train to anywhere.

Instead, she stayed caught in the emptiness he left for her to fill. It felt like freedom and choice. She wandered through it, examining flowers and trees, basking in summer's warmth, letting time flow by.

But a day came when he didn't leave the house early in the morning, and life suddenly wasn't so easy. He was in and out of the house all day. He worked in the yard and barn for a few minutes at a time, then back to the house.

She escaped early in the afternoon and stayed away until the sun was setting. He was sitting in the living room, staring out the window when she returned. He didn't look her at her or speak. His Adam's apple was bobbing violently like it did when he was upset.

She was hungry. She hurried to the kitchen, grabbed a piece of cornbread and cold bacon, then fled to her bedroom and locked the door. The next morning, he left early, carrying his food and water with him.

*

She dressed and walked to town. When she saw the buildings from the road, she turned and walked back to the farm. She couldn't stay in the house, so she wandered up to the knoll and sat beneath the oak tree.

She stared down at the house. How was she supposed to know what to do? Hidden in the deep shadows of her father's cruelty lay her mother's few good words, but they were weak, faded and thin, like her. They didn't fit the situation she was in now anyway.

She was his, yet she could never be his. He was hers, yet he could never be hers. Grady Miller's cruel legacy demanded that each of them live out life alone, their only companion, his legacy of hate.

But Fate had intervened, for they were together and married now. Two old children who never experienced a day of normal childhood or adolescence, or the usual young adult years that teach people how to love.

Neither one knew how to do this. It was that simple. Two old children searching for love. She shrugged bitterly and sighed.

*

He watched her climb the hill. He wanted to rush up the hill, gather her in his arms and crush her to him. He wanted to squeeze every drop of sweetness and warm bone marrow out of her. He wanted to have it forever fill the empty space he carried in every fiber of his being.

He wanted to rip her father's memory and treacheries away from both of them. He longed to throttle the thieving villains who'd stolen their love and hope and youth from them, leaving them old, without a chance.

He drew in a ragged breath and ran his hands through his hair. She belonged to him and would for eternity. They were married. That was a fact. Regardless of how it happened, they had traveled this far.

The only thing he knew to do was to distance himself for a while. Instead of going to her, he collected a few things from the house and carried them out to his little room in the barn.

*

The sun was setting. Nell stared down the hill at the darkened windows below. The lamps weren't lit. She wondered where he was. She waited while it grew darker, but the lights never came on. She went down the hill to the house, went inside, and lit the lamps.

Some of his things were gone. She peeked into his bedroom. His bedding was gone. She went out on the porch and stared at the barn. There was a crack of light coming from his little back room. He was leaving the house to her. She felt both pleased and dismayed that he understood exactly what she needed.

*

He didn't go back to the house except to get a few more things when she was out walking. He stayed away, leaving her to fight the battle within herself. He would interfere only if she tried to leave him. If she left, he would hire detectives to find her, and he would bring her home, by force, if necessary. She was his now, and he needed for her to become used to it. It was the only way both of them could survive.

Now he was a child back in the barn where he'd grown up, and she was a child in a farmhouse two counties away, both of them desperately trying to find a way to overcome the evil legacies stalking back and forth between the new house and the newly painted barn. The unrepentant, huge, hurtful Shadows of old man Smith, old woman Smith, and Nell's evil, lying father, who had kidnapped and murdered without conscience; their legacies of hate and evil hovered over them without surcease.

Another long week dragged by. Saturday evening came. He glanced at the house when he finished feeding the cattle. The lamps weren't lit. He went in the barn, fixed himself food and ate. Then he wandered back outside and glanced at the house again. It was still pitch dark, no lights on.

A frown crossed his face. Alarms went off in his head. He panicked. Had she hurt herself, or was she gone? He cursed as he pounded up the porch steps. He shoved the door open and rushed into the dark living room, breathing heavily.

He stopped and listened. He could hear her breathing. She was over by the fireplace, sitting in her rocking chair. The fire wasn't lit. The room was cold. After a minute, his eyes adjusted to the darkness. He felt his way over to the fireplace, knelt and fumbled for the matches and wood.

Then his big, rawboned hands went still. The darkness was familiar; it was the place where he'd been held captive most of his life. That was why it was dark in here. She'd been held captive in that dark place, too. Neither one of them had ever lived any place else when it came to other people.

Sympathy poured through him. Her life with Grady Miller had been just as poverty-stricken and cruel as his was with the Smiths. He gave a deep sigh and laid the matches down on the floor, sat down beside her chair and leaned against it. He felt her thin, trembling hand reach down and touch his face, a world of questions in it. He grabbed her hand possessively and ran it over his face. Then he turned it over and kissed her palm. She made a little sound of protest, and he made himself stop.

He knew what she didn't know yet, that they couldn't live without each other. They never had, anyway, looking back. He also knew she wasn't ready to accept that knowing.

He stayed still for a long time before she reached down to touch his hair, smoothing his infernal cowlick back from his face as though she was trying to tame the wild beast in him.

When her hand stopped, he knew the war in her had started up again. The war between the hate and the love they held for each other. They had both fought the caring growing steadily between them, but it stayed anyway, the lovely light of it growing steadily alongside the hidden, shouting wrongs. The wrongs that lived in this darkness.

"Forgive me," he said, "for so many things...."

She drew her hand away. He waited, for he knew he had to be the stronger one, the one who forged ahead, who said yes to them being together, for she was too afraid. She'd almost lost her soul already over what happened to her in life. He was never in danger of that; he would do this for them, he would keep this vigil. He would speak first. He would see to it they faced the darkness together this time.

"If there is a God, please help us," he murmured.

A long time passed. He rested his head against the rocker. He dozed off; she stirred. He woke instantly. He felt his way across the room and found the kerosene lamp. He pulled the globe up and lit it. The light fell across their exhausted faces. She stood up. He watched her walk slowly to her bedroom and shut the door behind her. He went to his bedroom. She was not going to be left alone in this house again. He crawled into his bed and slept like a rock.

The next morning, he was out of the house before she woke up. He stayed away all day. When darkness came, he watched the house. She didn't light the lamps again.

The brooding darkness drew him like a moth to a flame. She was waiting in it. He made his way into the dark house and sat down beside her chair. They waited together. She never moved. Finally, he touched her arm with his hand, laid his head against the rocker, and fell asleep.

Their routine followed the first night. The weather cooled and the fall days flew by, but he still did not light the fire to banish the darkness and give them the warmth and light they needed. Neither of them spoke of it in the light of day. He lit the fireplace in the early morning dawn, and they both warmed up in front of it.

Every night the coldness in the unlit, darkened living room grew. Then a night finally came when their cold hands fumbled for each other's in the darkness, and they held hands for warmth.

One night, a change in the air woke him. He was leaning against her chair, shivering in the cold. There was twilight in the room instead of darkness. He moved away from her, stood and went to the window. The ground was white. Large, lazy flakes of snow floated in the air. The first snow of winter was falling. Jubilation filled him. Winter was here at last, and with it, the coming of the white!

He turned to Nell, searching her sleeping face in the dim light before he sat back down beside her. He closed his eyes and slept peacefully. They'd stepped into the Light of their beloved Nature, the One who had faithfully companioned them growing up, who had saved their lives as children by sending them rain and snow and birds and rabbits and flowers. Nature was bringing Light into their darkness. Nature and the snow would do its work. It always had, forever more, amen. All was out of his hands. It was beyond his vigil now; he trusted Nature completely. A deep stillness surrounded them while they slept in the cold living room out on the old, isolated farm.

*

Nell woke up with a start. She gazed around in wonder. She could see in the darkness. How could that be? She looked out the window. Snow was falling. She looked down at him. He was asleep. She leaned back in her chair and closed her eyes. She waited, but the darkness didn't return.

The light outside kept getting brighter. She opened her eyes again and gasped in stunned awe as a beam of light poured through the window, carrying translucent, white outlines of laughing children and all kinds of birds into the room.

The children and the birds rode the beam of light into the room, dancing and flying around the two of them, grabbing and lifting and tossing the last worn out remnants of the evils that held their two souls in their iron grip most of their lives, flinging them into the beam of living Light.

She blinked as the laughing, dancing children and birds retreated back through the window, carrying the thin, tattered remnants with them. She watched them throw the remnants up into the snowy, dark night air. Birds of prey of all kinds grabbed the dark remnants and flew away with them like they were nothing. Then the children danced away, laughing with glee at the good deed they had done.

Nell sat still for a long time, inspecting the peaceful, empty space they left behind. After searching and finding nothing, she realized there was nothing left in their space except her and him. No more darkness. No more evil. No more Grady Miller. The Smiths. No more. Cross

Grove. All gone. They had come full circle. Their ordeal was over! The miracle they waited for through the dark, cold nights had happened.

The spirits of lost children without parents, homeless, but laughing, and Nature's birds, had danced through the snow and into the room. They'd carried away the ugly, shouting, protesting evils leftover from another era, an old bad time, through the window, and tossed them away as though they were nothing.

Tears flooded her eyes. Something tender moved humbly in her breast. Tears of awe and gratitude to God and Nature and lost children and their angels flowed down her face until she couldn't hold the sounds back. She buried her face in her hands and gave way to loud sobs of release.

He woke up and held her as best he could until her sobs died down. Then he climbed to his feet and pulled her up out of the rocking chair. She laid her head on his chest, and he wrapped his arms around her. She gave a great sigh.

"My Dear," he finally said in a mild voice, "should we put up a Christmas tree this year? It would be the first one for me....and you too? She nodded.

"We're late starters, but maybe we can help each other overcome the lacks we were handed, and move into the good places we were surely meant to live in.”

He glanced out the window at the falling snow.

“Maybe now we’re finally God’s children, too.”

She nodded. He pulled the pins from her silvery hair. He tucked her against his side and led her to her room. He turned back the heavy quilts and she crawled in, shivering. He covered her and turned to leave, but she motioned for him to stay. He climbed into the bed with her and pulled her close. She laid her head on his shoulder and sighed. Exhaustion and the warmth and softness of each other and the bed put them to sleep as soon as their heads touched the pillows.

The morning sun dawned bright and clear. Crisp snow danced in gusts over the farm. Sunlight poured through the bedroom window. Outside the window, the wind picked up and swirled across the empty yard, carrying the beginnings of a blizzard with it. The animals huddled together in the warm barn. The fire in the fireplace was ready to be lit, the sourdough starter in the pantry ready to be baked into hot, fragrant, crusty loaves of bread.

They both knew they would never sit together in the little white church in Cross Grove, for the townspeople wouldn’t stand for it. And, they didn’t want to. This was their sacred place. But they had each other now, and Claude and Margaret and Jason and Nola, a few others, and money to travel anywhere they wanted. And when summer came once more, they would sit together under the green cathedral made by the ancient oak tree up on the knoll above his farm, the place where they first saw each other, the place where it all began.

And from that place, together they would oversee the building of a bright new kingdom. A kingdom where no child got kidnapped, held hostage, their plight ignored, a place where orphaned children would never suffer the loneliness and emotional misery of being alone and unloved ever again.

The **E**pilogue

The Farm Boy and His Dad

We were standing out in the barn. I'd forgot all about Addition Jones until Dad mentioned his passing.

"How did he go?" I asked him. He got that same look I remembered from the day we'd been out in the barn talking about Old Add, back when I was a boy of thirteen.

"They found him in his little back room in the barn out on his farm. He was curled up on the floor, holding the bird books your grandfather gave him. They couldn't get them out of his hands because rigor mortis had set in, so they buried him with the bird books still clutched to his chest."

I remembered the story that ended years ago with the name, Nell Miller.

"What were you going to tell me about Nell Miller all those years ago?"

Dad smiled and said, "Yep, you still got a memory like an elephant. That's a good advantage to have in your line of work."

I didn't answer. We sat down on a couple of hay bales, and I stuck a hay stem in my mouth, sucked on it and waited, like I did back then when I didn't know enough to come in out of the rain. Back then I thought life would go easy for me, that my need to be wordy would take me to great and good places where I would be admired and revered.

Instead, I was back home for Mother's funeral, disillusioned and tired of trying to right wrongs, tired of trying to bring justice to the evils wreaking havoc in the world.

"Nell Miller lived a couple of counties away. She came to Cross Grove and told everybody that her father kidnapped Addition Jones and dropped him at the Smith's door when he was an infant. She said her father went back years later and burned the Smiths house to the ground with them in it.

Addition Jones had been gone for years when Nell showed up and told the town what happened. Cross Grove didn't like Nell telling them the truth. They felt guilty for leaving him to grow up with the Smith's, who shouldn't have raised a dog. They wanted to believe he'd murdered the Smith's.

Nell ignored them and cleaned up his farm and built a new house on it. Jones came back and found Nell and then his real parents, Jason and Nola Mennebar. It turned out his real name was Alexander Jason Mennebar. He wanted the town to call him A.J. Jones or A.J. Mennebar instead of Addition Jones, but they wouldn't do it.

So Nell and A.J. mostly stayed away from Cross Grove and took their business elsewhere. I guess they'd had enough of dealing with hate and evil. After a while, they started traveling. They traveled the world over, and in a few years, he came home without her.

Some ridiculous people around here speculated that he did away with Nell, as though there weren't laws in other lands, too.

A.J. told me and your mother and just four other people that Nell took sick and didn't want to die anywhere near Cross Grove. She loved Europe and wanted to die in Venice. Nell was cremated, and part of her ashes spread on the water there. The rest got spread around the little yellow house she built on his farm. He asked me and your mother, Jason and Nola, and Claude and Margaret to help him spread the ashes. He said that's what Nell wanted.

He stayed on the farm. Didn't travel any more. His mind got bad over time. Jason and Nola visited him as often as they could, and Claude and Margaret, too. Then Jason passed away, then Nola. Now Old Add is gone.

Only three of us are left to know that everything Jason, Nola, Addition Jones and Nell owned, and that was more than you can imagine, was left to Red Boggs, an orphan they raised, so he could start orphanages and take care of lost children. They planned it all out legal.

Red Boggs was eleven when Jason and Nola took him in and raised him. He was an orphan boy who lost his parents and a big bunch of siblings to an epidemic in New York City.

Boggs married and has a bunch of kids of his own, and he lives on Jason and Nola's big farm. He raises orphan boys on it, and they garden and farm and turn their hands to all kinds of things out there. They got a school and a doctor and programs for poor people, and a church for all kinds of faiths.

Boggs found a bunch of paintings in the barn on Addition Jones' farm. He found paintings of birds all over the barn walls, and canvases stacked everywhere. Addition Jones had painted them, and Red Boggs placed them with an art gallery in Chicago, and they are worth a fortune.

I heard Red Boggs plans to start a home for orphaned girls out on Addition Jones' old farm with the money from the paintings to honor Nell, and that's just a start on what is planned, with Boggs overseeing the future for them.

"Of course, people will talk," Dad said mildly, "but Boggs is a firebrand redhead who doesn't give a damn about gossip. Nobody tangles with him or his kids or his plans. He protects them all. Cross Grove knows he remembers how they treated A.J., so they just leave each other alone." Dad shrugged. "A standoff isn't always a bad thing."

I tossed away the stem of hay I was chewing on. We stood and left the barn and wandered over to my car. I studied the cold, hard ground and hefted my worn college suitcase still bearing travel stickers on it.

I had a human rights case to argue before the courts later on in the week, and I needed to focus on that. I would not ask him what he meant by any of it. Not right now. It sounded too much like him and Mother.

Now she was gone too.

No more cakes and pies. Now we were two men who would remain too solemn for the rest of our lives. Suddenly I remembered Mother feeding Addition Jones. I guess once there were three of us men who needed her instead of two. One old, one in the middle, and one young. I saw Addition Jones' loss when I was young but didn't know what it was. Three of us lost the good sweetness Mother and Nell kept in our lives.

A mournful wind interrupted my thoughts as though it knew what I was thinking. I felt weary, clear down to the bones, joints and knuckles of my life from fighting the evils human beings perpetrate on each other. I stared at the cold, windswept ground for a minute. I couldn't win. The wind gusted, nudging me out of my misery. I looked up at the sky and sniffed the air. Suddenly I grinned at Dad.

He nodded. Addition Jones and Nell had won their fight against an evil kidnapper and murderer, two damned old sinners, and a whole ornery, prideful town. Good had triumphed, and was spreading its wings over my childhood home. I couldn't ask for more.

The roots Addition Jones and Nell put down against all odds, would flourish in this part of the world, near the town that spurned them. Good does win over evil. I pulled Dad close in a hug of jubilation. We laughed together and sniffed the air like a couple of old hound dogs onto a new scent.

New snow was coming. It always came and covered the sins of the world for a while. The smell of it was sweet on the air, just like it was that day long ago when Dad was a young farmer explaining good and evil the best he could to his young son—back when I was a boy of thirteen.

About the Author

Patsy Stanley is an artist, illustrator and author. She has authored both nonfiction and fiction books including novels, children's books, energy books, art books, and more. She may be contacted at patsystanley123@gmail. for questions and comments.

More books by Patsy Stanley

Novels:
Addition Jones
An Older Wine
Emerald Hawks Flight
Avalon Blues Quest

Children's books:
Christmas Stories From the Crone's Castle
(author illustrations)
The Dreadful Noises of Landoshar
(author illustrations)

The Whuzzles

The Skaters

The Toy Car Series

The Christmas Story Series

Native American:
Red Leaf
The Green Mountain Shaman
Muse Art books:
The Zen of Three Zines
The Zen of Leota and the Laundromat

Metaphysics:
The Mental Body
The Spiritual Nature of Atomic Structure
Sound Energies

Shield Energies
Chakras, Meridians, and the Color Energies
The Elements

Avalon Blue's Quest

Avalon Blue, past sixty, hides the secret initiations holding her hostage, forcing her to remain a loner traveling the world in eccentric clothing of her own design. In Winter's Lee, a small northern fishing village, she meets Lucian and Melanie, cousins and best friends who have settled down, planning to be bored and lonely until their demise from old age.

That is, until an unexpected, muddy, squalling little messenger flings itself into their arms, bringing the gift of a new emotional, imaginative, journey involving Shamans, animal totem, tattoos and a mysterious island into their lives.

An inspiring, spiritually humorous story woven through with ageless magic, a story in which the never ending expansion of the soul meets love in daily life.